All About Marjory

All About Marjory

MARIAN CUMMING

Illustrated by David Stone Martin

HARCOURT, BRACE AND COMPANY
NEW YORK

To Emma Lee

*Who, like Emily, understands
and comes to the rescue*

Contents

1904

The gay young men drove two-wheeled gigs
And dashed around the town;
The ladies called in phaetons
And let the top part down.

For funerals and catching trains
We used the livery hacks;
For trips to town or streetcar rides,
The trolley on the track.

Girls poked in Shetland pony carts;
Boys cycled in a hurry;·
For picnics or just driving 'round
We filled the family surrey.

All About Marjory

CHAPTER ONE

Lost Child

"PICNIC IN THE PARK! Picnic in the park!"
Marjory Cameron chanted. She hopped up and
down on the horse block in time to her chant.
"It's almost a year since we had a picnic. I'm
so excited I can't keep still."

1

Papa was trying to pack the picnic lunch into the surrey and she was in the way. "You'd better be quiet," he said. "Old Whitey is patient but you don't want to fall under his feet."

Marjory stood still but her busy tongue ran on.

"Will the park look just the same as last year? Are there any new animals? Oh, Papa, do you suppose a child will be lost again? Remember the one last time?"

"My patience is nearly lost, young lady," grumbled Papa good-naturedly. "Here, I'll put the lemonade up in front and you get in and hold the jug steady and the jug may keep you steady." Marjory chuckled and scrambled up on the front seat. Picnics were fun! They were going to the City Park to hear the first of the summer concerts and they were going early to eat supper under the trees. Mamma came down the walk with Nancy and they sat on the back seat. Papa tucked the dust robe about Mamma's long full white lawn dress and Nancy's short stiff piqué coat.

They didn't need a dust robe on the front seat. Marjory's dress was a sensible "natural" linen that would not show dirt. But it was gay

with red and blue embroidery and a red patent-
leather belt that hung below her stomach. Her
light hair was in tight little braids turned
under with red bows, and her thin legs were
sensibly clad in ribbed stockings and tennis
shoes. Mamma had had almost eight years' ex-
perience with Marjory and she knew that she
was the kind of child that things happen to,
so she dressed her accordingly.

"Want to drive, Marjory?" asked Papa.
Marjory nodded happily. He handed her the
reins and leaned back. She sat up very straight
on the edge of the seat and held a rein tightly
in each hand. When she slapped them briskly
on old Whitey's back he stepped out smartly.
They rolled down the main street of the little
Texas town. Marjory hoped that someone she
knew would see her driving. The street was
wide and shaded with oak and magnolia trees
and the houses were set far back among the
trees. Other carriages were headed toward the
park. As they drew near, the street became
more crowded and Papa took the reins again.
Soon, above the trees, they saw the Texas flag
that marked the entrance to the park.

"Turn, turn here, Papa!" So Papa pulled

the left rein and they joined the procession of carriages going into the park.

"Go by the Animal House! Please! Please!" Marjory begged and Nancy echoed "Please!" from the back seat.

"We really ought to find a place to eat first. Oh, well, all right," said Papa, indulgently. He turned Whitey's head toward the old house that held the little zoo. In Bayou City's early days it had been a stately home; now, except for the graceful doorway with bronze lions on either side, little remained of its former magnificence.

"The lions are there to show it is an animal house," explained Marjory over her shoulder to Nancy.

"Lions inside?" Nancy asked.

"No." Marjory hated to admit that the zoo held nothing so exciting as a real lion. The cages were on the front gallery; they often held different animals. There were always, in some of the cages, squirrels and one or two sad-looking monkeys and a row of sleepy owls. It was always fun to see what else.

"There's something in the big cages," cried Marjory. She was stretched across Papa to see

4

better. "There's a bear! And what is that next to him?"

"A coyote," said Papa. "Some hunter must have caught him."

"Oh, drive slow! Drive slow!" she begged.

"What about your getting out? And we will go ahead and start eating," suggested Papa. "You won't care if you miss that, will you?"

For a minute Marjory thought he meant it. Her heart bumped at the idea of being nearer to the cages—alone. Papa's drooping mustache hid his smile but she could see the twinkle in his eyes. He was teasing again.

They drove past the central graveled circle where the bandstand stood with rows of benches around it. They did not stop there but drove to the picnic grove beyond, where people already were spreading tablecloths on the grass under the live oak trees.

Mamma immediately began spreading out the lunch and Papa went to tie up Whitey.

"Can I show Nancy the park?" asked Marjory. "She doesn't remember it very well." This was an excuse. She was the one who couldn't wait to see if everything was the same as last summer.

"Sure, if you're careful." Papa turned the surrey skillfully. "Keep her hand and keep your head. Come when I call."

"I will." Marjory felt very old and motherly. First they went to the little ravine that held the Brownie fountain. A statue of a wise, kindly-looking little Brownie held up a cup at just the right height for the children to drink.

"Want a drink o' water," said Nancy.

"Of course," replied Marjory, still being motherly. "But you must say 'Hello, Brownie' first. Everybody does."

They waited for a minute while some other children drank and said "Hello, Brownie," and patted him on the head and pulled his long nose.

" 'Lo, Brownie," said Nancy, and "Hello, Brownie," said Marjory. They both pulled his long nose lovingly.

"Look," said Marjory. "It's all worn smooth, but he's still laughing."

"It feels funny," and Nancy held her own nose to show how funny it felt.

They visited the little stream where the ducks lived and where the water fell over an old mill wheel. From there they could look

across at the monument to the Confederate
dead like a great quiet guardian of the park.

Papa's voice came ringing across the ravine
to them. "Marjory! Nancy! Come a-running!"
As they hurried back they could see people beginning to arrive for the concert. There were
families and couples walking. There were
young people on bicycles and farm wagons full
of children. There were pony carts with nurse-
maids driving and phaetons with gleaming harness and uniformed coachmen. These stopped
behind the benches so that the occupants could
listen to the music without leaving their carriages.

Marjory looked at the picnic supper Mamma
had spread on the red tablecloth. There was
fried chicken and stuffed eggs, potato salad and
tomatoes and pickles and olives. And there was
lemonade and chocolate cake. Then she looked
at the crowd arriving. How could they finish
in time? Before the others were through she
was standing impatiently, with her cake in one
hand and her glass of lemonade in the other.

But when they were ready they found seats
that suited them all, near enough for Mamma
to hear and for Marjory to see, yet far enough

so that baby Nancy, and perhaps Papa, could doze in the shadows. Marjory sat next to the aisle where she watched everything and listened contentedly. The concert was just as it had always been. There was the white bandstand, with its fretwork decorations, like a fancy iced cake. There were the bandsmen; the soldierly looking leader, the jolly drummer, the little man with the big horn. She felt they were her friends. The same grown people seemed to be on the benches and the same children running and playing in the paths and around the bandstand. The concert started with a Sousa march. As the other numbers followed Marjory began to be a little sleepy. Just then the trumpeter came forward alone. "Ta-ta-ra-ta-ta!" Marjory's eyes opened wide and she was alert at once.

"Oh, Mamma! How lovely! It's a Lost Child!" She gave a little wriggle of anticipation. At almost every band concert this happened. Some child playing in the aisles became separated from friends and was brought to the bandstand for the family to claim. It was like a play. The round white bandstand was the stage and the bandsmen, in their gold and white

8

uniforms, made a brilliant background. The
trumpet sounded again and the band leader,
slim and white-haired and elegant, stepped forward. He had a little girl in his arms and lifted
her to the railing of the bandstand. There he
held her, with a comforting arm around her.
Tonight the Lost Child was a tiny thing. Her
blond ringlets and long-waisted "French Dress"
made her look like a big doll. She wore a huge
pink hair ribbon and a wide pink sash and
through the fine lace and lawn of her dress
Marjory saw glints of pink. Sometimes the
Lost Child cried. This one was quiet, but her
big wide eyes showed how frightened she was.
She made an exquisite picture. An admiring
murmur went through the audience.

"What a charming child!" Marjory heard.
"She's like a big French doll."

"Poor little lost princess!" said Mamma.
That was it, Marjory thought, a little lost
princess!

"Ta-ta-ra-ta-ta," blared the trumpet again
and the bandmaster called, "Lost child! Lost
child! Anybody lost a little girl?" Marjory sat
forward. To have trumpets blown for you as
if you were a queen! To have the elegant Mr.

Lewes himself protecting you! It must be wonderful!

"I'd like to be a Lost Child," she whispered without taking her eyes from the rosy figure in the center of light.

"Don't even think of it, dear," said Mamma.

"Stage-struck," chuckled Papa.

Marjory was not listening. She was intent on the drama in the bandstand. Suppose no one came to claim the little girl! There was a sudden expectant silence over the crowd. Then a coachman in livery came up the path between the benches. When she saw him the Lost Child smiled for the first time and held out her arms stiffly and the bandmaster lifted her down to him.

"They should not have left her alone," said Mamma. "The children just run wild here. I can see why they get lost." The band music began again but now Marjory was restless. She was stirred by the excitement and felt there was something lacking in their picnic. She wanted to join the crowd of children who were "running wild" up near the bandstand. The faster the music grew, the faster they ran. *Dixie* had them scurrying like rabbits.

"Mamma, please, can't I go and play, too? Please!"

"I'm sorry, dear, but I can't let you go out in that mob alone," said Mamma. "If you see someone you know, that's different."

At that very moment Marjory spied the flash of a familiar green plaid near the bandstand.

"There's Emily!" she squealed. "See her green dress?"

Emily was Marjory's older cousin who lived with Grandma, but who was constantly in and out at the Camerons'. The children adored her as a delightful playfellow and their parents relied on her for she was a dependable fourteen-year-old.

"All right, run along. But come right back if she does not want you."

Marjory knew Emily would want her. She was already halfway down the path. As she neared the bandstand the green dress disappeared down a path on the other side of it. She followed as fast as she could. She ran out of the bright inner circle of light and the half light, and out into the big, dim park beyond the benches. But the green plaid skirt was surrounded now by other gay skirts and the longer legs of the big girls were taking them much faster than Marjory could go.

"Wait, Emily, wait for me!" she called.

She did not want to go back. She wanted to be with the big girls, so she trotted along behind them. They had come to the picnic ground. She knew the girls would have to turn back at the road so she sat on a bench in the midst of flying paper napkins and scraps from many lunches. She was glad to rest.

There! The girls had turned; they were coming back. She sat still in the dark, ready to say "boo" when they came to her. There came the green plaid dress. But it wasn't Emily at all! Marjory sat very quietly as the girls passed. They did not notice her. Their voices blended into the clamor up near the bandstand. Marjory sat thinking a minute or two in the quiet dusk. She would have to go back and sit down with Papa and Mamma and listen to the music like a grown up. She had promised Mamma that she would come right back. But she did not want to go alone through that gay, yelling crowd.

"I think I'd better go back the long way," she decided.

She began to stroll along in the shadows, keeping far from the crowd. It was nice out here. She could hear the band, delicate and far away. They were playing *The Anvil Chorus* and she could imagine how all the horns were blowing and how hard the little fat drummer was working. Out here it sounded like fairy horns. She could hear a mockingbird in the trees above her singing with the music. Against the stars the dim shape of the Confederate statue kept silent watch. He and Marjory and the singing bird had the world to themselves.

She moved along slowly for she hated to leave. She circled wide to stay in this pleasant, shadowy world. Suddenly her foot stepped, not on grass and leaves, but on nothing at all! Over the edge of a ravine she tumbled and rolled, with a gasp, to hard rocks at the bottom. As she rose to her knees she saw that someone was standing over her with his hand lifted as if to strike her. She crouched there, half up and half down, her heart beating quickly. Then she felt a trickle of water and caught her breath in a relieved sob. It was just the Brownie of the fountain with his cup held high! Just another friend, like the statue and the mockingbird. Marjory gave him a little pat.

"H-hello, Brownie," she quavered and reached for a drink of his bubbling water. The water splashed on the front of her tan linen dress. She felt better but she was still trembling a little. She realized, too, that she had come much farther than she thought if she was over here by the fountain. At least she knew now just where she was. She remembered that she had been sitting almost on the opposite side of the bandstand. She was farther back than she had thought but she kept to her intention of skirting the crowd. The music stopped; the intermission had begun. Running children were milling more thickly than ever, dashing down the paths and to the soda pop stand. Every now and then she dodged a shape hurtling past her. The paths that rayed out from the bandstand were a guide but she was afraid of the noisy, bewildering crowds that filled them. She kept to the grass. Her shoes were gray with dust now and the dark wet spot on her linen dress smelt like damp cardboard. Her braids slipped loose from their tight little rolls, as they always did when Mamma was not around to keep them tied. She gave them a little push up that did no good.

Now she had crossed two of the paths and reached the carriage road, which was plainer but dustier. The dark shadow of a building rose ahead of her and she realized that it was the Animal House! She had forgotten it. Within a few feet of her, in the dark cages, were a bear and a coyote! She wasn't in the surrey now, with Papa beside her and Whitey to take her quickly away. She was on the ground and the animals were somewhere near her in the dark shadows. A little more now and she would be past them—safe—could run, fast, to Mamma —to Papa.

She hoped the animals were asleep. She tiptoed. Quietly. Quietly.

"AHR—OOO! AHR—OOO!"

That terrible noise! Right in her ear! She gave a yell and ran fast—faster!—faster!— close now to the benches. Now she wanted to be near people—not alone in the night with wild animals.

She passed other children running. They were screaming in pretended terror in a game of catch. Marjory's terror was real but her screams sounded the same as theirs.

Just one more path now. She crossed the grass and dashed down the path. Halfway up and to the right, there would be Mamma's comforting arms and Papa's protecting presence. Her last steps were nearly flying, and then—and then—they were not there! No Mamma in her cool white dress, no Papa quiet with his cigar, no baby Nancy asleep on his lap. No, here was a big *fat* family, filling the space and spilling out into the path. They all looked at her as she stood there panting.

"Did you see my Mamma?" was all that she could gasp.

"No, honey, we didn't. And we've been sitting here all evenin'," said the fat mother, over her open picnic basket.

Marjory's mind whirled. Had she come up the wrong path or had Mamma and Papa moved? If this was not the right path, which one was? There were so many and she was *so* tired. She wandered in bewilderment down the path to the outside of the circle again.

It was just then that a long line of big boys playing "Pop-the-whip" dashed past. They rushed so fast that they did not see the little girl in the dim light. The leader popped the whip and the last boy snapped around the corner in a lurch that threw Marjory face down in the gravel. She sank behind the last bench, and sobbed in the dark. No one was on that bench so no one heard her cry and no one came to help her. Racing hordes of children were shrieking and shouting to each other all about her. It was lonely to be crying in the midst of a crowd and to have no one pay any attention at all.

Then someone leaned over her. "Vell, vell, vot's dis?"

She raised her eyes and saw the white-uniformed legs of one of the bandsmen. Her eyes traveled slowly up. Why, it was the drummer, the jolly little drummer who worked so hard and was always laughing. He wasn't laughing now.

"So, so, ve fix you," he soothed her. He helped her up and brushed the gravel from her face with a big, cool handkerchief. She clung to him and her sobbing was quieter. She still did not know where her family was but she was with someone she knew. She wasn't all alone.

17

"Are you lost, little one?" the comforting voice asked.

"No, it's my Papa and Mamma. They are gone!" The sobs almost choked her at the thought. "There is only a f-fat lady—and the coyote—and the Brownie scared me—and I fell down-n."

The drummer looked puzzled. "Don't cry. Ve go and find them." He picked her up in his arms. Then he noticed that people were going back to their seats. "No, the intermission is over. You come with me. I fix it."

She hid her face against the brass buttons and gold braid of the white suit. He hurried into the light, up the path and into the band-stand.

"Hey! Gus has another of them!" one of the bandsmen called to the leader. "Another what?" Marjory wondered. Then she was looking up at the resplendent leader himself. "Mr. Lewes vill take care of you now," said the drummer, patting her shoulder. He passed her over to the tall, white-haired man and made his own way to the drums.

Mr. Lewes lifted her to the railing of the bandstand. She stood there with her tired little

feet on the railing and her body braced against his white coat while his strong arm steadied her. Then suddenly the trumpet rang out "Ta-ta-ra-ta-ta."

That meant a Lost Child. Suddenly it dawned on her. *She* was the Lost Child! And it wasn't nice at all! It wasn't exciting. The picture of the curly-haired child flashed into her mind, all pink and white and doll-like. She didn't feel in the least like a princess. Her nose and chin were still stinging where the gravel had scraped them and her eyes were burning and swollen from crying so hard there in the dark. One hair ribbon was gone and her braid was slipping loose and her soft hair clung to her hot neck. Her stockings were wrinkled and one untied shoe string dangled over the edge of the bandstand rail.

But she didn't care! She didn't care! For there, coming down the path, was Papa, coming to get her. Oh, this was much better than being the Lost Child. Now she was Found!

CHAPTER TWO

Many Surprises

MARJORY AND NANCY were on their way to a party. Their crisp party dresses of embroidered linen, their ribbon-tied curls and their leisurely air proclaimed it. The June day was warm but the oak trees bordering the brick walk cast a cool shade. "They are like big parasols," thought Marjory. Each was amusing herself in her own way. Nancy rattled a stick along the picket fences as they passed and Marjory lingered to smell the flowers behind them.

"Is it a surprise party?" Nancy asked. Marjory sniffed vigorously. "Don't sniff at me!" Nancy frowned. "Is it?"

"I wasn't sniffing at you, honey," laughed Marjory. "I was sniffing all the flowers in Mrs. Bascom's garden. There are honeysuckle, and roses, and sweet peas and"—as they passed an oleander bush heavy with pink bloom—"oleander—all different kinds of sweetness." She came out of her cloud. "Oh, you mean is Miss Louisa giving a surprise party for one of the girls in our Sunday School class? No, she is just giving a regular party with a surprise in it. Don't you remember last Sunday she asked us to a party and then she said there would be a surprise?" Marjory tried to set things straight for her little sister.

"Nancy, I wonder what Miss Louisa's house will look like inside. It's like a big brick palace outside," she mused.

"Maybe kinda lonesome." Nancy was four but she did not stoop to baby talk. She was economical of words though, and it was surprising how she made a few do the work of many. Papa, who was a publisher, said that Nancy

22

had the makings of a journalist. She now added briefly, "What's the surprise?"

"I can't guess," said Marjory. "Maybe a Punch and Judy like they had at the church lawn party. Or a magician."

"Watermelons?" Nancy offered.

"No, if it was a watermelon party she would have told us to wear school dresses. Well, never mind! Let's hurry up and see!" and Marjory increased her speed with Nancy jogging at her side.

But as they drew near the imposing house where Miss Louisa Leonard, their Sunday School teacher, lived, Marjory's speed slackened. She always felt all mixed up before a party. She was eager for the pleasure ahead but it was not unclouded joy. For one thing, Marjory was a little shy. The Camerons lived near the edge of town and, while Marjory went to school and Sunday School, none of her classmates lived near her. For another thing, she was always afraid she would forget something or do something wrong. Mamma always told her not to forget her manners, not to lose her handkerchief or hair ribbon, not to be too noisy and to take care of Nancy. Marjory knew she was liable to forget or be noisy when she became excited and parties *were* exciting. Now she fingered her hair ribbon and sash, felt nervously for her clean handkerchief. She found that all was well, so far, and gained confidence. Nancy was either too young or too sure of herself to worry. She ran ahead up to the great dark door with its leaded panels of colored glass and rang the bell.

Miss Louisa herself opened the door.

"Hello, Nancy and Marjory," she said. "I'm so glad you have come. Now the party can begin."

Perhaps it was the light from the many-colored windows that made Miss Louisa look so gay. Her dark eyes were sparkling and her cheeks were as pink as her crisp pink linen skirt.

"You look pretty," announced Nancy.

"Yes," Marjory added. "You don't look like a Sunday School teacher at all. You look young."

"Thank you," Miss Louisa answered politely but her eyes twinkled. She led them into the big double parlors where the other girls of the Sunday School class were. They all had on their Sunday dresses and Sunday hair ribbons of pink

and blue. It was evident that they all had on
their Sunday manners, too, for they sat stiffly in
the parlor chairs of gilt and tapestry. Marjory
and Nancy sat down. They were all waiting for
the surprise. Miss Louisa smiled but she was
keeping the surprise until later.

The stiffness thawed as the regular party
games started. There was "Pin the Tail on the
Donkey," "Drop the Handkerchief," "Going
to Jerusalem" and "Farmer in the Dell." Miss
Louisa played the piano for "Going to Jerusalem" and the singing of "Farmer in the
Dell."

Perhaps one reason that Marjory did not remember all Mamma's reminders for behavior
at parties was because she played so hard that
she forgot that she was Marjory at all. When
they were "going to Jerusalem," she was not
marching to find an empty chair but was part of
some mighty procession. When she ran around
the circle in "Drop the Handkerchief," she felt
the tense excitement of the hunted. When she
was blindfolded to pin the tail on the donkey,
the feeling of blindness was so terrible that she
didn't care where the tail went in her haste to
see again. Each game left her a little less curled

and dressed up. Her handkerchief as well as the official one was dropped somewhere.

At the end of "Farmer in the Dell" she backed up to Miss Louisa who was sitting at the piano.

"Please tie my sash," she panted.

"Having fun?" asked Miss Louisa.

"Oh, yes," Marjory breathed. Then she confided, "I was so glad I was chosen for the Farmer's Child. I can't stand to be the Rat. I hate them."

Miss Louisa laughed. "I'm deathly afraid of them, too. Once I fainted in school when there was a tiny mouse in my desk. I'm glad you weren't one, too. You are a much better Child."

Marjory wanted to ask Miss Louisa if other grown people were afraid like that. If they were they never showed it. But just then a neat little maid opened the doors to the dining room and Miss Louisa struck up a march. As they formed in a line the girls' eyes met. Would the surprise come now? It still seemed like a birthday party as they marched in to the dining room and took their places at the table. There was no birthday cake but tall pink candles glowed in silver candlesticks and pink roses in a silver bowl took the place of the cake in the center of the table.

But there *was* something different. At each place stood a pair of paper dolls, the nice stiff, colored ones. And they were dressed like a bride and groom.

"Oh, how sweet! What lovely paper dolls! Thank you, Miss Louisa," they cried. But Pauline, the oldest girl, had a big sister who went to grown-up parties. "Sillies!" she said. "It's an announcement party. Look at the names on the card. 'Louisa Leonard' and 'Robert Whiting.' Miss Louisa is going to get *married!*" Her voice rose shrill and important.

"Married!" "A bride!" "Miss Louisa is going to be a bride!" That meant a wedding. With lights and flowers and wedding cakes! This was the surprise. They couldn't take it in at first. Then Marjory asked, quaveringly, "Will you still teach Sunday School if you get married?" The whole surprise would be ruined if she said no.

"Oh, yes, honey, just the same," Miss Louisa assured her. The other questions followed with a rush. They forgot their ice cream and cakes to crowd around her and ask, "How soon?"

27

"Will you have a church wedding?" And then someone remembered to ask, "Who is Mr. Whiting?"

Miss Louisa laughed. "Yes, a big wedding at Christ Church with 'veil and trail and orange blossoms.' Who is he? You know the Whiting Carriage Company?" They nodded. "That belongs to Bob's father. Bob has persuaded him to try selling automobiles. Bob will be in charge of the new department. We don't know when we will be married yet. It depends on whether the automobiles sell well or not. Bob thinks that some day they will sell as many automobiles as carriages."

Marjory wondered. There were a few in Bayou City, but she didn't know anyone who had one or had ridden in one. Automobiles were almost as exciting as a wedding.

The party was a complete success now. The children chattered about weddings and automobiles and ate their cake and ice cream with gusto. Miss Louisa looked at the chatelaine watch pinned on her shirtwaist.

"At five o'clock Mr. Whiting is going to take a customer for a ride in one of the cars," she said. "He always drives by here. Let's all go out on the front gallery and see them pass."

They trooped from the table and out onto the wide front gallery. Here they could look across the oleander bushes and down the shady street. There were a few carriages, a boy on a bicycle and a Negro in a rickety wagon, nothing else. At five o'clock exactly the quiet was broken by a loud "poop-poop" and a heavy chugging noise and the automobile came in view. It was a runabout, high and without a top, and Mr. Whiting and his passenger were very plain to be seen. The driver wore a cap and goggles but the customer was holding his stiff derby hat on firmly. Miss Louisa and the girls waved and Mr. Whiting lifted his gauntleted hand from the steering bar to touch his cap. There was another "poop-poop" and they were down the street leaving a cloud of smoke in their wake.

"He's just wonderful!" cried one of the girls. "And the automobile is wonderful, too!" said another. Marjory said slowly, "I know what he is like—Sir Launcelot on a fiery steed." Pauline laughed, "It's fiery, all right. All that smoke!" But as they went back into the house

Miss Louisa whispered, "I know just what you mean, Marjory."

In the house, as they began to say their good-byes, they were full of chatter and excitement. They were no longer the stiff little girls who had started out the afternoon. Going down the brick walk, Marjory felt her head spinning with all the new ideas. She was telling Pauline about the only wedding she had ever seen. It was Uncle Wynn's and Aunt Fanny's last year. It had been a small one, but there had been flowers and wedding cake and presents. Marjory made the most of it in the telling.

After Pauline turned off at her street, Marjory skipped along imagining a big wedding in Christ Church—like those in the *Ladies' Home Journal*, with candles and palms and white ribbons. Through the long summer shadows she strolled and turned in at her gate still in a dream. Mamma awakened her with a start.

"Marjory, where is Nancy?"

Where indeed? Marjory blinked. At what place in the afternoon's excitement had she lost track of her sister? She thought she remembered seeing Nancy at the table during refreshments, but what had happened to her since

then? Here she had thought she had behaved
well at the party and she had forgotten the most
important thing, to keep an eye on Nancy. She
drooped, all the elation of the party gone now.

"Oh, Marjory! Marjory! What am I to do
about you?" Mamma wailed. "How can I depend on you when you forget so? Now someone will have to go back for Nancy and dinner
is nearly ready."

The telephone on the wall behind her interrupted—two rings—their ring. She answered it
with her eyes still on Marjory's downcast face.

"Oh, yes, Louisa! Yes, she just came in. She
was? Oh, will you? I am so sorry you have to
bother."

"Miss Louisa says they will bring Nancy
home." Mamma turned and smiled at Marjory.
"She was still in the dining room, eating!"
Marjory relaxed and smiled back weakly. She
and Mamma went out and sat on the front steps
and waited. It was cool and dim and quiet.

"No great harm was done this time, Marjory, but you must learn to keep your wits. I
hope my baby wasn't frightened." Mamma's
voice grew soft.

"Mmmm," came from Marjory. It was

partly a promise to do better and partly a grunt over the absurdity of Nancy ever being frightened.

Suddenly the twilight quiet was broken. They heard a chugging and loud "poop-poop." Marjory was on her feet. Oh, no! It couldn't be that!

But it was. There came the automobile around the corner. High on the seat sat Mr. Whiting and Miss Louisa and perched on Miss Louisa's lap sat Nancy with her blue eyes shining and not a curl out of place. The first of anybody, of *ANYBODY*, to ride in an automobile!

Mamma and Marjory ran down to the horse block to meet the triumphant motorist. When Nancy had been lifted down, Mamma stood by the car, thanking Miss Louisa and Mr. Whiting for their trouble. Marjory and Nancy stood to one side.

"What was it like, Nancy, riding without a horse in front? Was it perfectly thrilling?"

"It was all right," said Nancy calmly, and then in an unusual burst of words, "And listen, Marjory, I had two great big dishes of ice cream!"

CHAPTER THREE

Hot Mud Pies

"IF YOU ARE going to play in the yard, Marjory," said Mamma, "I wish you would take Nancy with you. At least it is cooler out there. Pearl and I are going to be busy making those watermelon-rind preserves and she will be in the way."

"Oh, Mamma," wailed Marjory. "She's such a baby! I have to play baby games and give in to her all the time. Please don't make me! I want to make a lot of mud cakes and she'll just spoil things!"

34

"We are busy people, aren't we?" agreed Mamma with a smile that made Marjory's cakes as important as her own preserves. "Well, she's playing in the dining room with her blocks now. Run on, and I'll do what I can. Don't get *too* muddy and call when you are ready to come in and Pearl will turn the hose on you. One thing is sure, you won't catch cold on such a day! Whew!"

Marjory ran down the path and Mamma stood a moment at the back door looking out at the hot June morning. Already heat waves were dancing in the Texas sunlight. The mockingbirds were silent and only the jays called raucously. The air was shrill with the hot sound of the cicadas—"like grease frying" Mamma thought. The chickens were clustered in the dust under the fig trees, and old Doc, the collie, had found the spot where the water from the icebox dripped and was curled up there. The vegetables in the garden looked wilted and the yard was parched and dry. Where the ground was bare it was cracked in what the children called "earthquakes." Only the spot under the chinaberry tree, where the shade was deep and black, gave any appearance of coolness. Mamma sighed. Thick shade and "cakes" of cool earth and water seemed more attractive than the sunny kitchen behind her where the range was roaring and the preserves sending out clouds of spicy, sweetish steam. Pearl, the cook, didn't seem to mind it. She was singing at the top of her voice:

"When my blood runs chilly an' cold, I got to go,
I got to go, my Lord, I got to go.
When my blood runs chilly an' cold, I got to go
'Way beyond sun an' moon."

"No danger of anyone's blood running chilly and cold this morning," thought Mamma as she turned back into the kitchen.

Marjory hurried down the yard. She was afraid that Mamma might change her mind or that Nancy might demand to come. Since the afternoon of Miss Louisa's party she had tried to watch out for Nancy. But it was hard always to be the big sister. Today she had so many things to do. She had set up a bakery under the tree by the carriage house and she wanted to get to work at once. The chinaberry tree was low and wide-spreading. Under it the earth was soft and workable. She was going to make some really beautiful cakes for a big wedding like Miss Louisa's, and she did not want Nancy ruining things.

When she reached the "bakery" John Wilson was already there waiting for her. Marjory was glad, for there was no one she liked to be with more than John Wilson. Her family was somewhat curious when Marjory talked of playing with John Wilson.

"Who is this John Wilson?" queried Mamma one morning at breakfast. "Aren't you just talking to yourself? I never see anyone."

"No, she is there," explained Marjory. "She dresses like me and she acts like me, but she is *there*."

"She?" Papa put in. "Is John Wilson a girl?" Papa and Mamma did not often laugh at Marjory but they did at the idea of a little girl named John.

"She is! She is!" Marjory insisted. "She is a girl and her name is John Wilson and she is nice. She never laughs at me."

"Sorry," said Papa seriously but his eyes were still twinkling. "After all, if you create a person you have the right to call her what you choose."

"Huh!" said Marjory. Sometimes she didn't

37

understand Papa, but anyway she loved John
Wilson and was always glad to see her. She
didn't have much to say. Marjory chattered to
her and told her things that she never told anyone else; her "pretends," her plans and her
really important ideas. She was always willing
to play what Marjory wanted, but she too could
pretend and invent things. She was especially
good at baking, the perfect cook's helper, ready
with whatever was needed. Marjory was never
lonely when John Wilson was with her.

This morning she wore a brown Mother
Hubbard apron as Marjory did, with brown
barefoot sandles that would be shed as Marjory
became lost in the game. They started work at
once.

The tools were there from other mornings of
delightful baking. There were old pans for
mixing bowls, a baking powder can that served
as cookie cutter, and an assortment of bottles,
cans and discarded knives and spoons.

Marjory, like any good cook, collected her
materials before she started. There was a can
of water from the faucet over by the chickens'
drinking pan and a can of sand from the sand
pile at the side of the house. Papa had bought

it for Marjory and Nancy to play in, but it was poor stuff for real cakes and pies. It fell apart when it dried and was uncomfortable to handle. The good brown loam under the tree was much better. Sand was nice for sugar in cakes (in small amounts) and as a sprinkle of white on top of cookies. As she came back from the sand pile Marjory pulled off some heavy heads of Marechal Neil and Marie Henriette roses, to use for decorating.

"Now, John Wilson, we must work hard. We have a big order of cakes for that wedding," she said in a very important, grown-up tone. She sat flat on the ground with the mixing bowl between her knees. She was measuring the thick brown earth and water into it. The dirt was flour and chocolate, the water was milk or molasses. Eggs were a problem. Once Marjory had tried a real egg from the hen house but it didn't mix and was terribly messy. John Wilson had a better idea, so now they cracked imaginary eggs and separated them with a quick twist as Pearl did in the kitchen and then Marjory gave the bowlful of them to John to beat. This morning she debated whether she was making a cake or cookies, but decided on cookies because they were so much fun to cut. Then they had to be lifted with a broad knife blade and put on a board in the sun which served for the oven. Finally Marjory sprinkled them with white sand-sugar and pressed a red or yellow rose petal into the center of each. She and John Wilson stood, wiping their hot faces on their sleeves and admiring their work. "It's the prettiest batch of cookies we've ever made," Marjory boasted proudly.

Large cakes were best made in layers and they started a layer cake next. Marjory was mixing while John Wilson read her the directions and she did not notice Nancy as she came down the path toward the bakery. Nancy skirted the workroom itself and started picking up last year's chinaberries from the ground. They were yellow and soft and dropped without sound into the can she carried. The morning was growing hotter but under the tree it was still shady and cool. The soft dough that Marjory was working on was so attractive that she discarded the spoon and stirred it with her hands. It was wet and cool and oozed between her fingers deliciously. She happily sang a song that Emily had taught her:

Hot Mud Pies

"Tell me little housewife toiling in the sun,
How many minutes 'til the pie is done?

Johnny builds the oven; Katie rolls the crust;
Daisy finds the flour, all of golden dust.

Turn them so, and pat them so. What a dainty
size!
Bake them on a shingle. Hot Mud Pies!"

She interrupted herself to say, "Don't I wish
these really were for Miss Louisa's wedding.
Well, it's a big wedding anyway." So she chattered of weddings and presents and refreshments. Between the items she gave directions to
her helper.

"Please go see if the oven is hot enough.
Goodness!" she imitated Mamma, "that old
stove makes it hot in here! Now please hand
me the sugar, John. Oh, here it is." And she
reached for a can of sand. She was still sitting
on the ground with everything in a circle
around her. "One cup of sugar."

"Here are the raisins," said Nancy and
handed her the can of chinaberries. "Thank
you," said Marjory, with her eyes on the dark
mixture. "We will need some more to put on

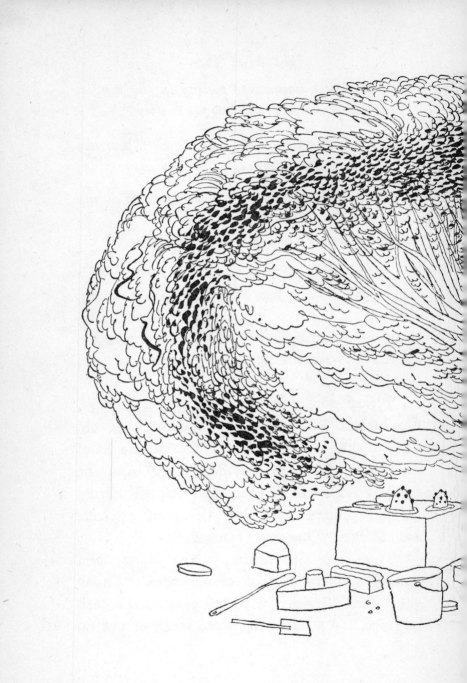

the top." Nancy trotted off and Marjory poured
the batter out in big round cakes. She would
pile them up for layers as soon as they dried a
little. Together, she and Nancy stuck the chinaberries in a border around the cake and made
a design of them in the center.

"You make another," ordered the head cook.
"I'm going to make hermits, with raisins."

"I'm going to make candy," said Nancy.
Marjory nodded inattentively and went off to
get more chinaberries. She was only conscious
that her baking was running more smoothly
than it ever had. There were rows of petal-
decked cookies, and the layers of the big cake
decorated with raisins, and soon she began drop-
ping little rough cakes of mud and chinaberries
on shingle baking pans, ready for the oven.
They were the best yet, just like Mamma's
Christmas hermits.

Nancy sat flat on the ground with a pan of
what was evidently chocolate fudge between
her knees. Her brown apron, like Marjory's,
was coated with mud but, like Marjory, she
was happy and unconcerned. Marjory went for
more water and when she came back Nancy was

marking out her fudge in squares on an old plate.

"Why, Nancy, that's smart!" cried Marjory. "Neither John Wilson nor I ever thought of that! You beat us both. When did you come out, anyway?"

"Long time ago," Nancy held up a broken corner of fudge for Marjory to taste as Mamma always did with real candy. Marjory nibbled the air near it in pretended enjoyment.

"I thought you were making a cake," said Marjory. To tell the truth she had hardly noticed that Nancy was there, she had joined the game so quietly. Like John Wilson, she had worked with Marjory and then had had little ideas of her own that she had carried out independently. But Marjory *did* remember something about a cake.

"John Wilson made it," said Nancy. "Look," and she pointed to a big bare space on the oven board. "Caramel."

Marjory looked and then looked quickly back at Nancy.

"Did you say *John Wilson* made it?" she asked.

"Uh-huh," said Nancy.

Marjory stared. No one else had ever treated John Wilson as if she were real. Most people just laughed at Marjory when she talked about her or else paid no attention to her at all. This was wonderful! She was playing with Nancy as if they were the same age. They had shared the fun and the work and the "pretends." It hadn't been "taking care of baby sister" or playing baby games. Nancy had had some good ideas; the fudge and the raisins. And now she was playing with John Wilson too! Marjory had a quick feeling of wanting to hug Nancy, but she realized that fitted the baby Nancy, not this competent little helper.

"John Wilson, honey," she said. "I hear your mother calling you. I expect you'd better run home. Nancy and I can finish up here."

CHAPTER FOUR

Little Jo

THE DAY THAT Grandma Cameron broke her hip, old Joanna Williams, her cook, sat down in the kitchen and cried. "I'm too puny to take care of her," she moaned. "Oh, Mis' Cameron, what am I gonna do?"

Mamma was distracted, too.

"I can't think yet," she said. "If even Emily were here. But I hate to send for her." Emily was visiting her uncle in St. Louis and seeing the World's Fair.

47

"Wouldn't be no good," Joanna fretted. "She's as flighty as your Marjory. My burden's too great, now." And her head went down in her apron again.

"We'll find a way later," and with a quick pat on the bent shoulders Mamma hurried in to Grandma.

After the doctor had come and gone and Grandma was resting quietly Mamma did think of a plan. "Joanna," she said, "you run over home and change places with Pearl. She's young and strong and can help lift Grandma, and you can look after Mr. Cameron and the children. I'll be over here most of the time. Will you, Joanna?"

"Well, if I do that," said Joanna, her old face wrinkled with anxiety, "I gotta have some help. That's a mighty big house and I ain't used to chilluns."

"All right, Joanna," Mamma agreed. "Who will you get to help you?"

"There's my grandchild, Little Jo. I could send up country for her. She's powerful smart an' could save me steps an' help with the chilluns."

"Yes, she would do," said Mamma. "Mr. Cameron can drive up Sunday and get her."

And that is how it happened that Little Jo came to the Cameron house. It was a lucky day for Marjory and Nancy. She insisted that she was the children's nurse and that they should call her "Mammy." As she was about twelve and as spry as a young goat and just as mischievous, this title tickled both Marjory and Nancy and they used it only when they wanted something from her. But as a companion she was utterly delightful and they could hardly bear that she should spend any time with Joanna. They hung around the kitchen until Joanna would explode, "Get out, all of you! I can't stand chilluns in my kitchen. Humph!"

Little Jo showed she was from the country by the old-fashioned way she wore her hair in braids. Her skirts were short and her legs long and her feet bare. She said she was in the fifth grade at home but Marjory and Nancy thought she was much better educated than Emily, who was in the seventh grade.

Little Jo taught them how to fish for doodle-bugs by spitting on a broom straw and poking it down dusty "doodlebug holes" and how to

49

make a daddy-long-legs point toward his home. She taught them to call to the charcoal man, "What you feed your wife on?" and was as convulsed as they when he called "Charcoal!" One day she called to a huckster that she thought was a charcoal man, "What you feed your wife on?" and he called, "Potatoes, tomatoes, okra, roastin' ears, cucumbers and watermelons." "That woman eat well," she chuckled. She took the children crawfishing down at the "Big Ditch" and when they got home cooked the tiny shrimplike fish and served them with vinegar and salt and pepper. And always she was singing or saying rhymes or telling them tales of her life in the country.

Mamma was delighted to have them so happy for she had to spend much of her time with Grandma. With Little Jo and Joanna to watch them she could feel perfectly satisfied about her little daughters. Little Jo sometimes did things in a queer way but she was quick and helpful and devoted.

One of her queer ideas was that she did not like to go to the grocery store alone. She always asked to take Marjory. She made a game of the errand. Marjory loved the game. Little Jo would come out of the house with Mamma's written list and whisper, "Orders from the General," and they would start quietly down the street. When they got out of sight of the house Little Jo would mutter, "General give me this to deliver. I'll allow you to help." When they reached the store she would look up and down the street and say, "I must watch here. Give this to the fat man when no one is lookin'." Marjory would take the list in her hand and tiptoe into the dark, fragrant grocery store. She would go to the end of the counter and hand it to old Mr. Schumacher and wait while he read it and collected the order. She was sorry that Little Jo did not come in for the grocer always gave her "lagniappe," a piece of candy or an apple for herself. She shared this with Jo when she came out, but if they had both gone in there would have been two apples or more candy, Marjory thought. Sometimes Jo changed the game and they were pioneers going to the fort for supplies with Indians lurking on their path; sometimes they were escaping slaves, buying food on the sly. It was always fun. And yet sometimes Mamma would say, "Oh, Little Jo, we're entirely out of matches," or "The grocer didn't send the onions" and Jo was off like a streak, just a little girl going to the store and nothing else. It was this unexpectedness of Little Jo that made her so attractive.

Nancy loved the way she read their picture books to them. She seemed so interested herself that she enlivened the stories and rhymes. "Looky, Nancy, honey, looky the big bear! Somethin' break his chair. Now wait, *here* she is!" The Mother Goose rhymes, when read by Mamma or Cousin Emily, were always the same but with Little Jo it was liable to be:

> *"Little Boy Blue, come blow your horn*
> *Your mammy keepin' your dinner warm."*

or

> *"Little Boy Blue, come blow your horn,*
> *You'll get chiggers, sure as you're born."*

And the stories she told "out of her head" kept both Nancy and Marjory openmouthed.

"You ought to write some of your stories down," said Mamma when she heard them one day.

"Oh, Mis' Cameron, I sure would like to some day," answered Little Jo.

"And I believe she will," Mamma told Papa later. "She seems so quick and clever most of the time. But then she will do something utterly stupid."

The next day was to prove one of the stupid days. That afternoon Jo and the children were playing in the small grove of live oak trees not far from the house. They were to come home when the afternoon train passed through. But before that happened, Mamma had an excited phone call from Pearl, at Grandma's.

"Mis' Cameron, I just gotta go to town. I got a terrible misery in my tooth. Could you or Joanna come over right away?"

"I was coming, Pearl. The surrey is all hitched. We'll both come, right away," Mamma assured her.

There was a confused scurrying around with the change of plans. Old Joanna moved slowly but finally she was ready and the things Mamma was taking to Grandma were gathered together.

"Here, Joanna," said Mamma. "Take these oranges and wait in the surrey. It's out front. I'll call Little Jo and tell her where we are." Mamma was flushed and flustered. Pinning her hat on as she went, she stood at the back door and called, "Jo! Jo! Marjory!"

She could hear and see the girls in the grove but they could not hear her. Snatching a piece of wrapping paper she wrote a hasty note in her large clear handwriting and propped it up on the kitchen table where they would see it when they came in. Then she went out where a grumpy Joanna was waiting. "That Pearl!" she muttered. "Running off with a misery. I'll take care of my old missus."

Not long after that the afternoon train whistled and Jo and Marjory and Nancy came in from "the woods." There was the note on the kitchen table. Little Jo went over it carefully. "Uh-huh," she grunted. "I takes care o' things." She handed the note to Marjory. "See how much *you* can read, honey," she said. Marjory found she could read quite a bit, Mamma's writing was so clear and familiar. There was *Grandma* and *Joanna*—she had seen these names written before—and there was *six* and *home* and *cook*, followed by a big word. "P-O-T-A-T-O-E-S," she spelled.

"Well, now you is comin' right along," said Little Jo. Marjory glowed with pride. "What she say is she an' Granny done gone to help your Grandma and will be back at six o'clock." She added impressively, "She wants me to cook a Poor Man's puddin'."

"Oh, can you cook a pudding?" asked Marjory.

"Sure, sure," Little Jo assured her and sat in thought for a moment. "Poor Man's puddin' is just a bread puddin'," she said as she reached for the cook book from the shelf over the table. She set Nancy to breaking up bread and Marjory to seeding raisins. She added kindling to the fire banked in the stove and opened the oven damper. Then she searched in the cook book and bent over the different recipes. "I likes a sweet puddin'," she decided and got out sugar and molasses and honey. When the bread was ready she measured and stirred and sifted, with quick looks at the recipe between times. She was very, very busy and seemed a little worried. But cooks were always worried, Marjory thought. She was delighted to be helping. Joanna and Pearl were so cranky about their kitchens that they "didn't want chilluns messing it up." Little Jo was different. When Marjory dropped the raisins, Jo just picked them up from the floor and dumped them in the pudding. An egg fell with a crash to the floor. Little Jo swept it under the sink. Mamma's note, on the floor now, was trampled in the mess underfoot and swept away too. She dashed in so much flour that it overflowed the bowl and sprinkled the table and floor. She used a great many dishes and piled them unwashed on table and sink. As the work progressed she scurried and scuttered around so that Marjory and Nancy were kept busy keeping out of her way. And she became cross—their happy Little Jo!

"Nancy, get out o' my path!" she fretted. "Kids in the kitchen, humph!" Marjory giggled. Jo sounded like Joanna. Jo glared at her. "Your Mamma told me to make this puddin'," she said sternly. "And I'm doin' it *right*."

When the pudding was mixed, it was too large for any pan except the big birthday cake pan. "What makes it so runny?" asked Marjory timidly. "That's 'cause it's raw," explained Little Jo. But her eyes were troubled. "I'll let Granny make the sauce," she said, wiping her hot face with her apron. "Let's go set the table while it cooks."

The table was set, the pudding was sending

out strange sweetish odors from the oven and the children were sitting on the back steps when Mamma and Joanna turned into the drive.

Little Jo was herself again. She grinned when Marjory said, "Won't Mamma be proud of your pudding?" But the grin faded as Joanna bustled into the kitchen and shouted angrily, "What you chilluns been doin' in my kitchen? I told you an' told you to keep out!"

Mamma was almost as disturbed. "What on earth has happened? What a mess!" She sat down weakly on the edge of a chair.

"I done made you Poor Man's puddin'," said Little Jo in a small voice. She hoped that this would bring peace. If the kitchen was mussed in carrying out orders perhaps it wouldn't seem so bad.

"Poor Man's pudding? Why on earth? What about the potatoes? I suppose you were all too busy playing to remember them." Mamma bent and looked in the oven. She saw the huge bubbling mass that certainly was not potatoes.

"Oh, scat, scat, all of you! I'll help Joanna. Sit on the front gallery and when Papa comes tell him dinner will be a little late."

Dinner *was* late. The children had time to tell

Papa all about their busy afternoon in the kitchen and the dessert Little Jo had made. There were no potatoes on the table that night but there were canned beans, which Marjory liked much better. Jo, a meek little shadow behind her grandmother, helped clear the table after the main course. Then Joanna announced grimly, "Mushmelon for dessert. Humph!"

"I think I'd like a dish of pudding," said Papa. "If you aren't saving it?" he politely asked Little Jo.

"Naw, sir. Yes, sir, Mr. Charley," said Little Jo. She flashed a grin at him and rushed into the kitchen. "You, Little Jo!" called Joanna, but, "Let us alone, Joanna," said Papa. "I want to taste that pudding." "Humph!" Joanna flounced through the swinging door. Little Jo came through it, in a moment, bringing a heaping dish of something black and smoking. She stood by anxiously while Papa tasted it.

"It tastes," he said slowly, "like caramel, and licorice, and burned toast, and omelet, and prunes, and tobacco. No tobacco in it?" he asked gravely. Little Jo shook her head. "Then I think that Marjory and Nancy may each have two small teaspoonfuls of it. The rest will be a treat for our white Leghorns." Jo's drooping shoulders straightened. Nothing was quite so bad when Mr. Charley could joke about it.

But even "Mr. Charley" found nothing funny about Little Jo's next misdeed, for this concerned his business and that was quite different from household affairs. He was expecting a very important telegram and thought it might be delivered to the house. He telephoned home in the middle of the morning. Mamma was out and Joanna was hanging up clothes, so Little Jo answered the phone.

"If a telegram has come for me I want you to open it and read it to me," he said in his hurried "business voice." Little Jo had seen Joanna receive a telegram for Mr. Cameron a short while before. It was lying on the card tray now on a little table beside the phone. She picked up the yellow envelope and hesitated a moment before she answered, "Naw, sir, Mr. Charley," she said slowly. "It ain't come. Yes, sir, if it do, I'll let you know." She hung up the receiver.

Mrs. Cameron came in the front door just in time to hear Little Jo's reply. She saw her standing there with the telegram in her hand. "Little Jo," she cried, "what is the matter with you?

Give me that telegram! Get away from the phone!"

That night, as she and her husband sat in the living room after dinner, they discussed Little Jo's sins. "I'm just as provoked and upset about it as you are, Charley," said Mrs. Cameron. "She said that she was sorry, but there's no possible excuse for such a thing. This is too much. I can forgive tricks and messes and foolishness but not lies. Now I can't be sure of anything with her. I thought she was just stupid but this is really dangerous. She can't be trusted with the children."

Mr. Cameron's voice was puzzled. "I just don't see it. Why on earth should she lie about that? Just reading a telegram! It must be just cussedness. Well, honey, get a good nursemaid and let Jo go back to the country. This summer has been torn up with her monkeyshines." This was an exaggeration but he was upset and vexed with Little Jo.

"The children will be heartbroken," hesitated Mrs. Cameron. "She really is wonderful with them. Look at them now."

They looked across the hall into the dining room where three heads were bent over an open book. The large colored glass shade over the table light hung low, its border of purple grapes, red apples, and yellow pears glowing and gleaming like jewels. In the circle of light beneath it Little Jo's dark head showed above Marjory's fair braids and Nancy's sleek curls. Little Jo was writing and the children were watching her intently. "I just can't send her away," said Mrs. Cameron.

"This here bride," Little Jo was saying. "She is Miss Louisa Leonard." She paused to write. "And the big fat man with a pipe, he is Mr. Schumacher." Again she wrote. "Who is the fairy queen?" asked Marjory. "Who? Her? That's me, Joanna Leconia Williams," said Little Jo with a giggle, and wrote with a flourish. "Here, I finished your scrapbook, Marjory. Now, I'm going to do Nancy's."

"I can't read your writing very well," said Marjory.

"That's fifth grade writing," declared Little Jo quickly and bent over Nancy's book.

Marjory slipped quietly down from her chair and came into the living room. In the hall, coming in from the kitchen, was old Joanna, ready to go home. She had her hat on over her bandanna. She was bringing the basket of silver to Mamma before she left. She reached the door of the living room and stood there waiting as Marjory took her book to Mamma and laid it open on her lap.

"Read it for me," she said. "What does it say?"

"Why, it doesn't say a word! It's just scribbling! Joanna, why *does* Little Jo do these things? Look, she has scratched and scrawled all over this scrapbook!"

"Oh, Mis' Cameron, ma'am, I thought you knowed. Little Jo can't read or write."

There was a moment of incredulous silence. Mamma spoke first. "But, that can't be," she protested.

"Yes'm. She is terrible 'shamed of it. You see, all the rest of her fam'ly does. But they moved to the country just 'bout the time she should'a started school and they warn't no colored school nigh there. I thought you knowed or I'd a told you."

"Oh, Joanna, you should have!" said Mamma. "This explains so many things."

"Jerusalem!" breathed Papa. "Poor little

kid!" He got up and quietly closed the door to the dining room.

Marjory looked from one to the other of the grown people with puzzled eyes.

"You see, Marjory," explained Mamma, "Little Jo has been trying hard all summer to keep us from knowing her secret—that she can neither read nor write."

"But she is in the fifth grade," objected Marjory.

"That was just part of her pretense," said Papa. "And we thought she was stupid! Stupid! She read your picture books with her own rhymes because she couldn't read the real ones. She took you to the grocery because she was afraid Mr. Schumacher would ask her to read the lists. She lied about the telegram because she couldn't read it and she bluffed magnificently when she thought Mamma had written her to make a pudding."

"I could cry when I think of that pudding," said Mamma.

"We should all cry when we think how near we were to sending her back to hopeless ignorance," fumed Papa. "We must do all we can for her. Marjory, you must help us keep her secret. Joanna, can she live with you in town if we help out? There's a good school near here that she can attend and no one need know what grade she goes into."

"Oh, yes, sir! She surely could! Thank you, sir! I think Little Jo will do you proud. She's plenty smart!"

"But, Papa!" protested Marjory. "If all the nice games were to hide that she couldn't read, will reading spoil her? I like Little Jo as she is!"

"I think that we can safely say, Marjory," said Papa solemnly, "that nothing, not even reading, will spoil Little Jo's charm."

And Papa was right.

CHAPTER FIVE

The Perfect Doll House

EVERYONE HAD SPOKEN of it as a perfect doll house from the first. Marjory had wanted one for a long, long time but somehow felt that it was a dream that would never come true. Each year she wrote *Doll house* in her letter to Santa Claus or her list of birthday "wants" but nothing came of it. Then just before her eighth birthday in June things began to look more hopeful. Papa asked, "Would a four-room doll house be large enough?" And Mamma said, "If you had a doll house, it would be nice if the wallpaper were like our own, wouldn't it?" Marjory had never thought of these details but she agreed. She didn't care what it was like just so it was a doll house.

For weeks before her birthday Papa seemed very busy. Every night after dinner he would go over to a neighbor's house and come home tired but full of secrets. Sometimes he would make unexpected remarks like, "Red houses are stylish this year," or "Lace curtains are nice, don't you think?" Mamma laughed at that. She was very busy too, sewing on things that she hid if anyone came near, and she would not take Marjory with her when she went to town. Marjory became more and more sure that there would be a doll house for her on her birthday.

And, sure enough, there was a doll house! It was so big that the pointed roof reached almost to Mamma's shoulders. Marjory stood stock-still and looked and looked. She didn't notice any of her other presents. The house was bright red and there was a gold curlicue on one of the gables. There were four rooms; downstairs were kitchen and dining room, and upstairs were par-

lor and bedroom. The wallpaper was like their
own but it was like their ceiling papers, with
tiny designs and soft colors. Rugs and curtains
and even the quilts on the bed bore a faint re-
semblance to ones in the larger house.

Nancy was delighted with it too. "Look,
Nancy," breathed Marjory in delight. "Look at
the cunning kitchen. It's my favorite. Look at
the little stove and icebox and all the little pots
and pans. And the colored cook doll—just like
Pearl! And the cat by the stove! Isn't it sweet?"

But Nancy liked the bedroom best. Nancy
always had ideas of her own. "Teeny baby doll!"
she chanted.

"Yes," Marjory said. "The baby in the cradle
and the Mamma doll in front of the little bu-
reau. It's a darling room."

But she liked the dining room too, with the
table set and the Papa doll with his black
mustache and shiny hair standing by the window. The parlor had a piano and fireplace and
two little girl dolls on the sofa.

That afternoon Mamma gave her a party.
Eight little girls came and Marjory was very
proud as she showed them the doll house. She
loved to point out the tiny things. Each time she

found something she had not seen before. The
mothers would say, "I never saw such a *perfect*
doll house!" and "Perfectly lovely! There isn't
a thing left out." The little girls all said, "I
wish I had one just like it."

Papa and Mamma were as proud of it as
Marjory. Papa pointed out how well made it was
and Mamma showed the doll's clothes and the
curtains and the quilt.

The next day Marjory wanted to undress and
dress the dolls in the doll house. She never felt
that she owned a doll until she did that. But the
lovely clothes were sewed on!

Mamma said, "Oh, Marjory, let's leave it as
perfect as it is for a little while! Undress your
old Mary Jane. You must be very careful of your
doll house. Not many little girls have one as
nice as this."

So Marjory played with her old dolls. She
wanted them to visit the dolls in the doll house
but they were too big. They could not sit in the
tiny chairs and even when they sat on the floor
their feet stuck out and kicked over a table. So
she pretended that the old dolls were taking a
walk in the garden. She was not really playing

with the house but she played around it and
looked at it lovingly.

It was strange but Marjory enjoyed the doll
house most when they had company. The other
little girls and their mothers would praise it and
admire it and Marjory was very proud and happy
then. But when she was alone and tried to settle
down and play regular games with it she could
not think of things to do. She could move the
dolls from room to room and dust and straighten
furniture. But the doll house did not need to
have a thing done to it. It was too perfect.
More and more she played with other toys.

One day Mamma told Marjory, "Papa is
afraid you don't like the doll house. He says you
never play with it. He is quite disappointed."

"Oh, Mamma, I do like it!" Marjory ex-
claimed. "I love it. It's just perfect."

That night after dinner while Papa was reading his paper Marjory played with the doll
house. It was still in the parlor where it was con-
venient to show visitors. Marjory knelt in front
of the doll house and seemed to be having a very
good time. If Papa had really watched he would
have seen that she was just playing at playing.
She talked for the dolls and moved them around

but she was very gentle and careful not to hurt anything. Finally she thought she had played enough. She said in a loud voice, "Now you must all go to sleep. Good night, all of you."

Papa looked up from his paper and smiled. "Pretty good, eh? You really like it, don't you?"

For a minute Marjory felt as if she were Papa's mother and he were an eager little boy. She said, tenderly, "Oh, Papa, it's wonderful! It's my perfect doll house."

Every night for a week she played a while in front of Papa. She wanted him to know how she loved the doll house.

Then Mamma decided it took up too much space in the parlor and it was moved up to the little girls' room. Now Marjory could stop playing in front of Papa. That was getting pretty tiresome. And she and Nancy could make up games better when they were alone.

One day when Mamma and Nancy were in town, Marjory was dusting the doll house dining room and had all of the furniture out of the room. Tiger-Kitty, Nancy's little kitten, looked in at the dining room window.

"Help, help!" Marjory called in mock terror. "There's a tiger looking in the window."

Marjory hurried the Papa doll up to the parlor
with the little girl dolls and put all the dining
room furniture up there too. Tiger-Kitty looked
into the dining room. Then he went in and
sniffed at the curtains. Marjory pushed the fire
screen in front of the dining room and yelled,
"I have captured a tiger. I have captured a man-
eating tiger!"

All morning Marjory played zoo. Tiger-
Kitty did not mind at first but soon he wanted to
get out. He clawed at the windows and tore the
curtains. He tried to climb the walls and tore
the paper. He acted just like a real tiger! Marjory was having so much fun she forgot to
notice what he was doing to the house.

"Oh, Marjory!" said Mamma when she
came home. "Your lovely doll house! You
should have known better."

But the damage was done. The dining room
was ruined so Marjory put the furniture on the
closet shelf and used the room for all sorts of
games. The toy animals gave a circus there and
the paper dolls moved in for awhile. The other
rooms were still perfect and Marjory kept them
as nice as ever. It was rather as if a gypsy band
had moved into a stylish neighborhood.

The Perfect Doll House

After Grandma's accident Mamma had too much to do to worry about what happened to the doll house. And, of course, Little Jo came to live with them.

One day old Joanna, with Little Jo's help, was cleaning the children's room and she accidentally crashed a chair leg through the kitchen window of the doll house. She made the children stand aside while she cleaned up the broken glass and saw that there were no sharp pieces left in the window.

"Can't have you cuttin' yourself while your poor Mamma so worried," she muttered. "There, now, it's clean as a whistle."

Marjory could put her arm right through the window now. This reminded her of something. She cleared out the furniture and pushed her head and as much of her body as she could into the kitchen. Her hand and arm stuck out of the window.

"Nancy, look!" she called. "I'm Alice in Wonderland in the White Rabbit's house. Send Bill the Lizard down the chimney!"

"We haven't any chimney," objected Nancy, reasonably. "And I haven't any lizard."

"Well, then get some cakes and drop them on

me. That's what the little animals did to Alice."

Nancy found some animal crackers and dropped them on Marjory. Marjory called out, like Alice, "If you do that again I'll set Dinah on you!" Then she ate the cakes and pretended they were making her smaller. Then Nancy was Alice and Marjory dropped cakes on her. It made a good game. They did not put the kitchen furniture back. They put it on the shelf of the closet with the dining room furniture. Now they had two rooms to play in.

The dolls in the rooms upstairs still lived their orderly lives. Instead of standing by the dining room window the Papa doll stood by the parlor window, and the cook now sat by the baby doll's cradle. They must have been surprised at the life that went on below them. At first the children pretended that the lower rooms were flooded and that the family had moved upstairs for safety. But they soon forgot all about them. Little Jo had joined their games now and added her own peculiar spice to their make-believe. The lower rooms became in turn a grocery store, a pioneer fort and a fire station. One rainy day Little Jo discovered that she could put a pillow on the peaked roof, and by climbing on a table she could mount it like a horse. "I'm a-riding a horse!" she called out. "Oh, let us ride!" shouted Marjory and Nancy. "This here is my horse," claimed Jo. "But I tell you—play like I'm a livery-stable man. You can hire my horse for five minutes for a pin." They all took turns, including the livery-stable man. They rode miles and miles that afternoon and Jo's dress front bristled with pins. The house stood it well. Papa had been right when he boasted that it was a well-built house.

One day the man came to stain the bedroom floors. To make room for him Joanna took all the furniture out of the doll house and with Little Jo's help put it out on the upstairs gallery. It was laid on its back with the open side up. The three children looked at it, speculatively. Anyone could see that plans were forming in their minds.

"It's not a house now," said Nancy.

"It's a ship!" announced Little Jo. "A little red ship!"

"A little red ship with a gold figurehead!" added Marjory.

It did look like a ship, with four little compartments instead of rooms, and the pointed roof with its gold ornament was like the prow of a ship.

"All aboard!" said Jo. "Ship goin' to sail. Get in, everybody! I'm captain!"

Marjory and Nancy climbed into the two lower rooms that were now the back compartment. By tight squeezing they could sit down in them. Jo was too big to sit. She stood up in one of the front rooms and it became the captain's lookout. With an old tin horn for a spyglass, she looked far down the summer street. "All aboard for Europe and Gal-*vest*on and New Orleeens!"

It was a wonderful place to play. They put the rest of the doll furniture and the little dolls themselves on the closet shelf and forgot about them. All the rest of the summer they played on the cool gallery where the breeze from the Gulf swept freely. Sometimes the doll house was upright as some kind of a building, sometimes on its back as a ship and sometimes on its face as a platform for plays. The red paint turned pinkish and the golden decoration showed white plaster underneath, and the remaining windows looked dingy. But Marjory and Nancy were enjoying it more than ever—much better than when it was

new. But they never thought of bringing anyone to see it now.

When summer was over and autumn had come, everyone seemed to settle down. Grandma was much better and Emily came home from St. Louis in time for school. Joanna, with Little Jo, went back to her small house in Grandma's yard. Little Jo started to school in a brand new plaid dress and red sweater and Marjory went back to her school. She was in the second grade now. Mamma was home more now, for Grandma could spare her, but she was very busy catching up on duties that she had had to neglect during the summer. She did not seem to notice the change in the doll house. After school and on Saturdays Marjory and Nancy played happily together now and she left them alone. With the first cool winds the doll house was moved back into the house.

One day soon after, Mamma came into the room where they were playing. She seemed to notice the dilapidated condition of the doll house for the first time. Today it was the Alamo and Nancy and a gallant band of paper-doll Texans were holding it against Marjory and the invading domino Mexicans.

The Perfect Doll House

"Would you like to have Santa Claus fix up your doll house for Christmas?" she asked. "It looks terrible. I didn't realize how bad it was. He could repaint it and freshen it and replace any missing furniture. Would you like that?"

For a minute Marjory and Nancy both looked as if they were about to cry. The mere idea was like a blow. They did not want a doll house that was so pretty that they could not play with it. Or namby-pamby dolls that had to be kept just so! They wanted one that could change with the flash of their own ideas—that could be a zoo, or a ship, or a fort, or a hospital at will. They cried out together, "Oh, Mamma! Please, please don't change it! It is *just perfect* now!"

Mamma looked at the poor old battered doll house and laughed and laughed. She laughed harder and harder when she thought of the spic and span house it had been and of all the work that had gone into it. The little girls watched her wonderingly. At last she wiped her eyes. "Of course, darlings, I understand. It shan't be spoiled. It really is a perfect doll house!"

CHAPTER SIX

And Glory Shone Around

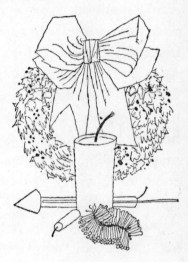

"I DECLARE," said Aunt Fanny, looking out at the Southern night, "I'm really homesick. This doesn't seem a bit like Christmas time. When we left St. Louis it was snowing hard."

She was standing at the window in Mamma's room. Marjory was sitting at Mamma's feet while Mamma rolled her straight, fair hair on kid curlers for the great day. She tried to turn to look at Aunt Fanny but a gentle tug on her hair restrained her. What did Aunt Fanny mean? Why! It was *just* like Christmas! There wasn't any mistaking the feel of it.

"So warm, not even frost!" Aunt Fanny's crisp, quick northern voice went on. "Windows wide open—and roses. And those terrible firecrackers!"

Mamma laughed. "I think it *is* mostly homesickness, Fan. You've mixed the good and the bad of a southern Christmas in one jumble. As housekeeper, I'm glad when we have a Christmas warm enough for us to do without fires and for the children to be out of doors. I'm used to the firecrackers."

Already Marjory was only half listening. Grownups just didn't *know*. Talking about fires and roses and housekeeping when tomorrow would be CHRISTMAS! Even everyday things like the uncomfortable kid curlers, took on an exciting meaning. When those curls were taken down it would be Christmas morning!

The house was full for not only had Aunt Fanny and Uncle Winn come down from St. Louis, but Grandma and Emily had come over from the other side of town. And Joanna and

Little Jo were visiting Pearl and helping her in the kitchen.

When Mamma finished her hair Marjory stole out to the top of the stairs and looked down into the wide hall below. The bannisters were twined with smilax and holly and the red glass shade of the hanging lamp in the hall was hung with mistletoe. On the big double doors to the front gallery there were holly wreaths with red satin bows as wide as sash ribbons, Marjory thought. She leaned over the rail and stretched on her toes to see if the parlor door were open and if she could get a glimpse of the tree. The door was closed but she could smell the pine mixed with the odors of spice and sage from the kitchen. She sniffed and shivered with excitement and then went quietly to their pink and blue room where Nancy was already asleep. When she was in bed Mamma came and tucked her in. She left the door open a crack that made a friendly angle of light and allowed all the unusual Christmas noises to come in. Emily was to sleep in here on a cot. Marjory hoped that she could stay awake until Emily came to bed. Marjory never saw enough of Emily though she often spent week-ends with them. She told wonderful stories and it was fun to snuggle down beside her when Nancy was asleep and whisper together.

Then all of a sudden it was morning and Emily was sitting up on the cot opposite and drawing on her robe. "Is it time to sing?" whispered Marjory. The room was gray and cold.

"Yes," said Emily. "We've had a little norther. Put on your slippers and robe." She went to help Nancy with her robe. Marjory fumbled into hers and then the three, with shivers that were more excitement than chill, stood outside the door of Mamma's and Papa's room and began to sing, quaveringly,

"God rest ye, merry gentlemen,
Let nothing you dismay——."

Inside they heard a grunt and a groan from Papa. "Lordy, Lordy, it's started!" but in a minute his tenor voice and Mamma's clear whistle reinforced their piping,

"And its tidings of comfort and joy."

The children called "Merry Christmas" and went on down the hall to serenade at other doors.

By this time odors of coffee and the little pork

sausages that were part of the Camerons' Christmas breakfast began to come from the kitchen. And from the kitchen too came Little Jo, up the stairs, shouting, "Christmas Gift! Christmas Gift!" to anyone who might hear her. She dashed in and helped Marjory and Nancy into their clothes, combed Nancy's real curls and Marjory's kid curler ones and, in spite of the excitement that permeated them all, got them down to breakfast just as Pearl brought in the coffee. Marjory and Nancy could hardly bear to turn to the right into the dining room, instead of to the left into the parlor, but Mamma was firm about "breakfast first." With the sausages and the tangerines, it wasn't so bad to eat breakfast but Marjory wished that grown people would not stop to talk. They even took second cups of coffee! At last Mamma put down her napkin and smiled at the impatient little girls and the waiting was over.

It was here! Now! The long-awaited. The very tiptop of the whole year. Heart, be still! Eyes, open wide! Breath, wait an instant! Silence, while the folding doors slowly are pushed open!

In the darkened room shone the lights of the

tree, ruby and gold and sapphire and emerald; jewels reflected in other jewels of glass and tinsel and spun glass. Scent of pine and oranges and sachet and chocolate and peppermint! Great stacks of mystery tied up in red and green and silver! Glimpses of toys under dark branches or atop the mysterious packages. A moment of speechless wonder. Then each child made for her own stack marked by her bulging stocking.

"My doll! My doll!" and Nancy ran straight to her child. "Oh, Mamma! The St. Nicholas!" breathed Marjory, getting a glimpse of the magazine's cover under her stocking. The tide of Christmas rushed in with the hiss of tissue paper, with confusion and noise and dizzy joy. "Oh, looky, looky, Mamma!" "Here, let me cut that string." "Oh, Fan, just what I wanted!" "Where shall I put this?" "Nancy, Nancy! Mine's pink!" "Look out, Marjory! Don't step on those dishes!" "Dig in the paper. There ought to be another cup." "Oh, grand!" "Christmas Gift!" "Little Jo, here's your stack!" "There comes Mrs. Martin up the walk." "Go to the door, somebody. My lap is full."

Neighbors came and the gifts from them must be opened and the present for them searched out from the pile on the piano. "No, no, Emily, that's for George. Mrs. Martin's is flat and long." The noise of a mouth organ and a toy piano almost drowned out Papa's new Harry Lauder record. And everyone shouted above all the noise.

Then, imperceptibly, the tide began to ebb. Mamma and Aunt Fanny, still looking for the missing cup, began picking up tissue paper. Emily started salvaging ribbons. Nancy retired to a corner by the tree with her doll. Marjory piled her presents on the couch, lovingly examining each one. At last all was in order. The parlor looked more like itself again and less like a cave of enchantments. A queer feeling came over Marjory. She nibbled some candy and peeked into the *St. Nicholas*. She blew a dispirited squeak on the mouth organ and whizzed the spinner of one of her games. She put on the embroidered apron that Grandmother had given her and her amber beads and sprinkled herself with cologne. A string of lights went out on the tree and she stood looking at it vaguely.

Then Papa turned off the victrola. Very deliberately he lighted his cigar. But he looked as excited as Marjory had felt when she saw the tree. Why, of course! Marjory remembered. Firecrackers!

"Nancy! Firecrackers!" she screamed. Papa reached under the tree for a handful of packages of firecrackers and "stompers." Nancy and Marjory scrambled into sweaters and then followed him out on the front gallery. "Come on. Come on," he called. "Come on, Little Jo. Come on, Emily, you aren't too grown-up for firecrackers." Emily followed and sat dignifiedly in the porch swing for a while but was soon down on the steps with the rest. Papa separated a bunch of the little firecrackers for the girls. One at a time they lit them at the glow of his cigar and threw them out on the lawn. They stamped on "stompers" that made long, phosphorus-smelling streaks on the sidewalks and sounded like a package of firecrackers. With a glorious abandon Papa himself shot off whole packages of firecrackers at once. Every so often he would send the squealing children up on the porch while he set off a "baby giant." They pretended to be terribly frightened and covered their ears in delighted terror at the gorgeous noise.

The boys across the street were shooting their firecrackers and so was someone in the next

block. The cool air was full of the exciting smell of phosphorus and powder. Marjory sniffed it eagerly. This was a different Christmas—sharp and tingling and invigorating. Indoors, around the Christmas tree, all had been soft and warm, sweet and confused. Mamma's Christmas, thought Marjory. This was Papa's. Cold air, sunshine and the exciting popping of the "crackers." His enthusiasm set theirs afire just as his glowing cigar lighted the firecrackers. They squealed and shouted and stamped and banged. At last they were tired and sat on the bottom step amid the wreckage but Papa reached in his pocket for one more bunch.

At dinner Aunt Fanny spoke again of the firecrackers. She had just come from church and the noise and the scent of the explosions had followed her all the way home.

"It seems such a terrible way to celebrate the birth of Christ, with gunpowder and noise," she said, in her quick, decided voice. "Christmas is holy and the music of the Christmas carols should not be drowned by warlike sounds. It should be celebrated with dignity and piety."

"And over-eating and over-drinking and indiscriminate giving and receiving," said Papa, with a rush of words, and then, catching Mamma's eye, added, "Nothing personal, Fan. Have some more turkey."

"Celebrations are queer anyway," commented Mamma. She saw that Aunt Fanny and Papa would never agree on this. "Why does football express our thanksgiving to God for his mercies, or crowded, noisy watch-parties the start of a clean New Year? It is the feeling behind the celebration that matters."

"And besides, I LIKE FIREWORKS," declared Papa, like a stubborn little boy, "and Marjory would leave home if we didn't have our sky-rockets tonight. She's a terrible heathen." He smiled at her troubled, wide-eyed gaze.

After dinner Marjory and Nancy tried dutifully to take the nap that Mamma had ordered. Naps seemed a terrible waste of time and Marjory thought that she couldn't bear it if she didn't have the fireworks tonight to look forward to. But she fell asleep almost as soon as Nancy did.

Late that afternoon Papa took Grandma and Joanna home and then took Nancy and Marjory to a carol service at the church. Marjory loved the church at Christmas with its lighted candles and shining star above the altar and red-tied holly wreaths. She loved the music the choir and the children sang. As they drove home in the blue dusk she tried to tell Papa how she felt about the music.

" 'Oh Come All Ye Faithful' and 'God Rest Ye, Merry Gentlemen' and 'Hark! The Herald Angels Sing' are like the church. Like red and gold. 'Oh, Little Town of Bethlehem' and 'Silent Night' are like it is now. Like blue and stars."

Papa slapped the reins on Whitey's back and looked down at her. "Not bad," he grunted, "not bad at all—for a little heathen."

That made Marjory think again of the discussion at the dinner table. She wished Papa hadn't reminded her because all afternoon when she thought of it she had been troubled by Aunt Fanny's remarks. She wondered if it *were* showing disrespect to the Baby Jesus to have fireworks. With a baby you wanted things to be quiet and soft and restful. Candlelight and songs. She had never thought about it before. There was no use asking anyone because this seemed something on which even grown people disagreed. Suddenly she was glad she didn't have to decide. After all, the fireworks were under the tree, waiting for them. She gave a little jump of joy. First supper and then the fireworks.

Supper was glasses of milk and turkey sandwiches. Then at last it was really dark. Papa and Uncle Winn were bringing out the fireworks. There were sparklers that Nancy and Marjory could have at once. They waved them and danced with them. They looked like some sort of fairy celebration. Mamma and Emily and Aunt Fan sat in the porch swing and each held a sparkler. Their faces were like bright masks in the light. The pinwheels were fastened to the fence and sometimes went off in a blaze of glory and sometimes refused to turn or burn at all. Papa and Uncle Winn and Emily and Little Jo shot the Roman candles with their falling stars and balls of colored light but only Papa and Uncle Winn shot the skyrockets. There was one fire balloon that rose and floated like a wandering planet into the blue distance.

Papa allowed Marjory to shoot one Roman candle while he helped her hold it. It was an astonishing feeling to be in the midst of those falling stars and colored lights as the fiery balls shot high. One minute the world was emerald green, one minute electric blue, one, glowing

red. She could hear the family exclaiming
"ooooh" and "ahhhh" as the color changed.
After that sparklers seemed babyish and weak,
so she retreated to the horse block. Here she
was near enough to the glamorous wielders of
the fire and yet safely behind them and out of
their way.

This was like sitting in the front seat at a
play, only better, because whichever way she
looked there was a different scene. The sky
above was deep azure. Behind her, where there
were no lights, she could see the silver stars
picked out against that blue. Down the walk
shone the yellow light from the front door with
a glitter from the Christmas tree mixed in. It
shone on the red satin ribbons of the holly
wreaths and on the red sweater flung across
Mamma's shoulders and the plaid of Aunt
Fanny's cape. It was the home light, warm and
rich and familiar.

But the lights from the fireworks in front of
her were rare and heavenly. They were like
nothing else in this world. It might be like this
in the middle of the Milky Way. Colored
planets rose and fell, the starry shower continued. At times a rocket rose like a comet,

swift and smooth and aspiring. Marjory's spirit ascended with it, joyous and vivid and wondering. There was something about it of glory.

"And the glory of the Lord shone 'round them."

Too vague for words the feeling enveloped her. The blue southern sky. Shepherds in wonder at a bright light. Angels singing in celebration. She needn't have worried. Fireworks were just like Christmas!

CHAPTER SEVEN

Ferry Tale

"NOTHING EVER HAPPENS between Christmas and Easter," Marjory grumbled to Emily. "Just rain and cold and school. And now Nancy is in bed with that cold. I'm glad you felt thirteen today." She grinned across the work-strewn dining room table at Emily who was painting paper dolls for her. It was a joke in the family that Emily never was her real age of fourteen. Some mornings she woke up feeling fifteen and wound her dark braids around her head. On those days she went with older girls and talked about clothes and boys and parties. She even sat rocking and embroidering and chatting with Grandma or Mamma. But when she woke feel-

ing thirteen, her braids were down her back
with a big bow at her neck and the gap between
her and eight-year-old Marjory was not so
great. She smiled back at Marjory.

"Doesn't promotion to the high second grade
help any?" she asked.

Marjory was cutting out a paper doll just
then and her tongue always stuck out and wig-
gled in time with the scissors so she just shook
her head. They had several old copies of
Mamma's *Delineator* and were cutting out and
painting all sorts of additions to Marjory's
paper doll family. She finished cutting and said
crossly, "It's just more school."

"What is your paper doll family named?"
Emily asked, trying to find a more cheerful
subject.

" 'Leonard' for Miss Louisa Leonard. Nancy
wanted it too, but she took 'Whiting' for Mr.
Bob Whiting. I wish Miss Louisa would get
married now instead of waiting until spring.
That would be exciting."

"She explained that." Emily dipped carefully into the always scarce crimson lac paint.
"Mr. Whiting is selling automobiles all right,

but shipments have been slow so they have had to wait."

"Uh-huh." Marjory was cutting again. Then she laid down the scissors so that she could say with emphasis, "Well, something nice has just got to happen!"

"We might try magic," Emily lowered her voice in a way Marjory loved.

> *"Double, double, toil and trouble,*
> *Fire burn and caldron bubble."*

Marjory giggled but half believed in Emily's magic.

And then she wholly believed in it. Mamma came in with some mail and said, "Aunt Annie wants us to bring you and Marjory to Mardi Gras this year, Emily." Both girls gasped.

"Mardi Gras!" Marjory squealed. It was like an invitation to wonderland. "Oh, Mamma, can we go? Can we?"

"Do you think we could?" Emily said quietly but just as eagerly.

"I'll talk to Papa. And to Grandma," said Mamma slowly. "If Nancy's cold is better she could stay with her there—" She smiled at

97

their waiting faces. "It really might be managed. Don't depend on it, but we'll see."

There was no use in trying to paint after that. "I'm going home and talk to Grandma right now," said Emily. "You clear up, Marjory."

Marjory put away the paper dolls and emptied the gray paint water. She felt as if she were walking in a golden mist.

Mardi Gras in New Orleans! Mamma and Papa went there often to spend that magic week before Lent began. They came back with tales of balls and parades and maskers. Aunt Annie's young lady daughters, Cousin Ada and Cousin Nettie, sent party favors and souvenirs for Marjory and Nancy—paper hats and artificial flowers, shining pins and frilly fans and once even a cloth-of-silver ball gown. Papa and Mamma brought back papers with colored pictures of the floats in the parades, lovely and grotesque. All this was in Marjory's mind and she almost prayed that she and Emily could go.

After many phone calls and talks it was finally decided that they could go, and questions burst from Marjory as she followed Mamma around.

"Oh, Mamma, will we see the kings and queens? How many are there? Can we see all the parades? Will we sleep on the train? How long does it take? And—and—and"

Mamma laughed. She knew how Marjory felt. After years and years of attending the New Orleans Mardi Gras she still had the same thrill of excitement.

"You will see as much as we can manage for you. Certainly the Comus parade on Mardi Gras night. The kings each have their own parade, Rex, Comus, Momus. Cousin Ada and Cousin Nettie will have to tell you about the balls. But you will see enough to make your eyes pop— fairies and giants, castles and dragons, silks and jewels and cloth of gold. It will set you dreaming for months to come."

Mamma was sorting the clothes they would take. She put her long white gloves and opera glasses on the stack. The sight of them made Marjory realize that it was true; they were really going.

"But when will we get there? How long do we ride on the train? All night?" Marjory squirmed over the foot of the bed as she watched

Mamma's quick sorties into drawers and boxes and closets.

"Yes, all night. We cross the river early in the morning and get to New Orleans in time for breakfast with Aunt Annie." Mamma was on her knees now, among the shoes in the bottom of the closet.

"A river?" Marjory queried. She had never seen a river.

"Yes, of course, the Mississippi River. The ferry will take us across." Mamma was reaching for boxes on the shelf and did not see the amazement in Marjory's eyes.

"Do you mean a real fairy?" Marjory gasped. F-e-r-r-y and f-a-i-r-y sound much alike and she had never heard of a ferryboat. And all the tales of wonder of Mardi Gras made a helpful fairy not too extraordinary.

"Yes, honey." Mamma had settled down now and was running ribbons through corset covers. She thought Marjory was talking about the ferryboat. "It really is wonderful. I'll never forget the first time we went over. The ferry takes us over—train and all! Marjory, run down and ask Pearl if she has ironed your best petticoat and I'll put fresh ribbons in it. I want your things to be just so on this trip."

"Train and all? That's magic, isn't it?" wondered Marjory.

"It does seem that way," said Mamma. "Hurry up and don't start dreaming now. You and Emily will see it all soon."

Not dream when she had so much to fill her dreams! She did her errands in a daze and then went in by the living room stove and sat alone trying to realize it.

"A fairy! I'm going to see a fairy!" She had almost given up all hope of seeing a fairy and was beginning to doubt if there were any. And here Mamma was saying quite seriously that a fairy would take them across a river. If Papa had said it Marjory would have known he was teasing but Mamma always told her the truth.

Nancy came in still sniffling from her cold. Marjory felt sorry for her because she was not going to Carnival too. But she had to talk with someone about it. "I'm going to New Orleans, and listen, a *fairy* will take us across the river."

"Huh," said Nancy. "I'm going to stay with Grandma. Grandma lets me stay up till nine o'clock!" No one ever had things better than Nancy.

Marjory sat with her chin in her palm, looking at her scuffed shoe toe. No wonder Mamma wanted everything right. When you are going to see a fairy you want to look your best.

In the days before they left she was very helpful. She made no objection to shampoo and kid curlers. She got out the big suitcase and dusted and polished it. She ran errands happily, and, most wonderful of all, she didn't forget what she was going after.

"Marjory is improving," said Mamma.

" 'Just 'fore Christmas I'm as good as I can be,' " quoted Papa with a grin.

In a way it was like before Christmas to Marjory. It seemed that the days would never pass. But like the days before Christmas they finally did.

The enchantment began when Papa and Mamma and Marjory and Emily entered the hushed green Pullman car. Most of the berths were already made up. Emily and Marjory shared one and lay snuggled together in the dark, whispering and watching the lighted towns slide by in the night.

When they peeped out of the window the
next morning they could feel that the country
was different. The gray Spanish moss on the
trees was longer and thicker than in Texas and
at the bases of the trees were bushy little palms,
like palm-leaf fans. They watched a while and
then Emily took Marjory down the swaying
aisle to the dressing room and helped her dress.

However, Emily felt fifteen that morning
and primped for a long time so Marjory left
her and sat with Papa as they drew near the
river. There was much starting and stopping
and backing and shouting of brakemen. Sometimes she could see the water and then they
would shift and it was out of sight. At last Papa
said, "Want to go outside?" and she nodded
eagerly. The train seemed to be on a platform
by the river and Marjory looked eagerly to
catch the first glimpse of the fairy. She watched
the trees on the shore. Perhaps the fairy was
waiting there. Then she glanced down and saw
that a band of water had appeared between
their platform and the bank and it was widen-
ing. She turned puzzled eyes to Papa's face. He
smiled down at her.

"Well, how do you like your ferry ride?" he asked.

"When does the fairy come?" She waited breathlessly.

"Oh, *this* is the ferry," Papa slapped the rail of the platform on which the train stood. "I know it looks like a big bridge but, see, it is moving. It's lots better than the old ferry. We had to get off the train and catch another on the other side. This boat takes train and all."

Marjory thought she was going to cry. This ugly old boat instead of a glamorous fairy! "A fairy," she said and then was silent.

"Sure," said Papa. "One of the largest ferry boats anywhere. Sometimes they are rowed by hand. There was a poem in McGuffey's—

> *"A chieftain to the highlands bound*
> *Said 'boatman, do not tarry*
> *And I will give you a silver pound*
> *To row me o'er the ferry.' "*

Papa loved to quote from the old McGuffey's reader that he had studied as a boy. He went on through the whole long poem. Marjory was glad that he did. It gave her a chance to choke back her disappointment and hide her face. She looked hard at the trees along the shore. She should have known better, she told herself. She shouldn't have expected a fairy in everyday life. She would not let anyone know how silly she had been. She sniffled in the early morning wind and straightened her shoulders.

" 'Come back, come back,' he cried in grief
  Across the stormy water
 And I'll forgive your highland chief,
  My daughter, Oh my daughter!' "

Papa finished with a flourish.

"And now 'my daughter, Oh, my daughter,' if you are starting to sniffle, we'd better go sit in the train with Mamma and Emily. Then New Orleans and Aunt Annie and breakfast. Then Ho! for Rex, king of carnival, and Comus and his Mystick Krewe!"

Marjory sniffed again but it was partly a sniff of disdain. He wasn't going to catch her again! She knew now that there were no kings and knights and Mystick Krewes. They would turn out to be another dull grown-up thing. She would never again believe anything they told her. She climbed into the seat beside Mamma and looked drearily out of the window. Her heart was as dull and sluggish as the gray river they were slowly crossing.

Aunt Annie's house was in a bustle of excitement when they arrived. They sat long over a late breakfast making all sorts of plans for the days ahead. This was going to be fun, anyway. Marjory was entranced. But as the day wore on she felt worse instead of better. The sniffle she had on the ferryboat turned into a real cold and the disappointed lump in her throat turned into one that hurt. Finally Mamma noticed her silence and her flushed face. She put a quick cool hand on Marjory's forehead.

"Fever," she said anxiously. "Oh, honey, you must have caught Nancy's cold. Annie, I am so sorry. We should not have brought her."

"She won't be any trouble," said Aunt Annie easily. "We'll put her to bed in the front bedroom and old Chloe can take care of her. But the poor baby! To be sick at Carnival!"

It wasn't a bad place to be sick, though, Marjory found. She lay in the great carved walnut bed with a camphor-soaked rag around her throat, sipping hot lemonade. Everyone was so sorry she could not go out that they did all they could to make up to her. She saw all the party dresses and watched Cousin Ada and Cousin Nettie depart in a swirl of ruffles and gusts of excitement for the balls. Sometimes Papa and Mamma and Emily went with Aunt Annie as spectators and sometimes they went to the parades in town. From the balls they brought gay programs and favors and from the parades they brought candies and souvenirs, badges of the carnival colors, purple, green and gold, balloons, and funny masks.

"Marjory, you are so good about staying home," Emily said as she was leaving for the Proteus parade. "I would fuss terribly about it."

Marjory didn't tell her that she didn't really care. She still didn't believe much in the glory she was missing. It was like the long tales old Chloe told her about other Carnivals, lovely but unreal.

She did hate missing the maskers on Mardi Gras morning, for though she was much better Mamma did not want to take her in the crowd. "But you shall see the Comus parade tonight dear," she said. "And it is the loveliest of all."

In spite of her determination not to let her hopes rise too much about the parade, Marjory was all a-tingle on Mardi Gras night as they waited for it. They were not in the crowds on the sidewalks but on a gallery overlooking the street. A friend of Aunt Annie's had a shop where the parade passed and had invited a party of his friends to see the parade there. Papa found a place for Marjory at the corner of the railing where she could see far down the gaily lighted street. Both street and sidewalks were filled with the expectant crowds. Some were trying to stay in place to watch the parade and some in groups and lines were pushing their way through, all good-natured and noisy and excited. Hawkers called their wares, street bands of little Negro boys played and danced and people of every race and age and costume surged along. Every so often there would be a cry of "Here it comes!" Then the milling crowds would stop and necks would be craned toward the end of the street. Marjory would stand on tiptoe and gaze down the street too. But each time there was disappointment and more waiting.

She was getting sleepy. She yawned loudly. Papa turned. "Don't go to sleep before you see the Mystick Krewe," he warned.

Marjory roused. "What does Mystick Krewe mean?" she asked.

"The parade is given by Comus and his Mystick Krewe. It's a very secret club. No one knows who Comus will be. I have seen a lot of their parades, and I feel as excited as you do. It's magical!"

"Magic again!" Marjory thought scornfully. "Grown ups!" She thought of the bleak moment of the ferry crossing. It wasn't Papa's fault but she wasn't going to be caught again.

Then suddenly he grabbed her arm and pointed down the street. "Look! Look! The red glow in the sky! Here comes the parade!"

Marjory looked and saw that indeed the sky was red. Far away she heard the sound of trumpets. She forgot her disdain and jumped up and down in anticipation. The crowd heard it too and surged forward with a roar of excitement. The parade as it drew near looked like a brilliant serpent. First came the heralds and members of the Krewe on horseback. Their cloaks of blue and silver and red and gold blew in the wind as they rode. "They are like the princes in a fairy book," said Marjory wonder-

ingly. "Look how their horses prance and the jewels on their harness!"

The horses that drew the lumbering floats were covered with long robes from head to tail and the Negroes who led them looked sinister in robes and hoods.

"They look scary like Genii from the Arabian Nights," whispered Marjory fearfully.

"Yes, or Moors or Turks," Papa added. "But look at their faces and their feet."

Marjory did and felt better. Their faces were good-natured and below the robes she could see overalls and heavy workshoes.

Other robed Negroes carried flaming torches that lighted the floats. And the floats themselves glowing in that flickering light against the black of the night!

They were unreal, beautiful, terrible, with kings and giants, temples and grottoes, a winged ox, a fire-breathing dragon. The torchlight glistened on gold and spangles and jewels and threw dark scary shadows on jagged rocks and caverns. On each float, dwarfed by the huge figures and monsters, were live people, splendid kings and knights, ladies and goddesses. They danced, they bowed, they threw kisses. Their masked faces were blankly insipid but they were splendid and dashing.

"This one on the first float is Comus himself," explained Papa. "The others are members of the Mystick Krewe."

Marjory nodded without looking up. She saw that the Krewe were flinging something besides kisses to the crowd. Long paper serpentines floated out and were caught with eager hands. Some of the Krewe threw candy and bits of gaudy jewelry. Marjory held out her skirt and an elf on a high tower threw a handful of candy into it. This was fairyland indeed! Another called to Papa and tossed a string of gold-colored glass beads. Papa caught them in midair and dropped them over Marjory's hair and around her neck. "A gift from Comus." She tried to thank him but a band playing a Sousa march passed below and he couldn't have heard a word.

Bands, floats, floats, bands! Each time Marjory was afraid that this one was the last and then another would lumber up and another magic world would be spread out for her; gay, beautiful, awesome, splendid. Finally the last glittering bower passed and she looked beyond and could see no lighted scene behind it. She watched its shining beauty as long as she could see it. Then she looked up at Papa still following the fading glow down the street with the same longing eyes as hers.

"What happens now?" asked Marjory.

"Comus and his Krewe go on to the ball and we grown people too, after we take you home. If you are lucky you will dream about it. Tomorrow is Ash Wednesday. And New Orleans will sweep up her streets and go to the cathedral and the Krewe will begin to plan for next year's parade."

"I'm coming back," cried Marjory, "next year, and the next, and the next—" Her eyes were shining like the beads around her neck. "It *is* like magic, Papa."

The next morning, their bags loaded with favors and gifts for Nancy, they caught the early train for home. When they came to the river it was Emily and Marjory who stood outside on the ferry while Papa and Mamma sat inside in the train.

Marjory had thought she could never tell anyone about her mistake and her disappointment on her first ferry ride, but now, after the enchantment of the Comus parade, all that seemed small and unimportant. Emily gave her shoulder a quick intimate squeeze as they stood together and Marjory said impulsively, "I want to tell you something, Emily, if you won't laugh." Then she told her all about it.

"I was silly, but I did think Mamma meant a *real* fairy," she ended.

"No, not silly," said Emily, her eyes on the water lapping past. "I suppose growing up is like learning to live in a foreign country. You have to learn new ways. You are bound to make mistakes. I remember when I was little I thought a horse doctor was a horse that doctored other horses!" Marjory giggled.

"I still make mistakes sometimes," Emily confessed. "But you just have to ask your way around. I've been here in Grown-up Land a little longer, so you can talk to me and I won't tell."

Marjory squeezed her hand.

"Well, at least I know there aren't any fairies at all," she said sadly.

"That *is* silly." But Emily smiled. "Just because you made a mistake doesn't prove there are no fairies. Even if you never *see* them, it's no proof that there are none. They are shy and want to live to themselves. But they leave traces; tracks in the dew, wishes granted, a kindness done, even gifts sometimes. Why, Marjory, I once heard of a fairy who—"

Marjory sighed happily and watched the western shore coming nearer and nearer as Emily began her story.

CHAPTER EIGHT

The Stolen Dream

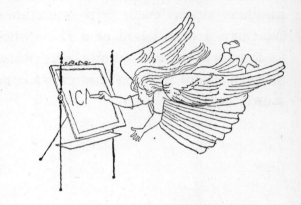

MARJORY SAT UP sleepily in bed and thought about the wonderful dream. Her mind was a misty tangle of candlelight and flowers and her adored Miss Louisa was in the center of it. She snuggled back into her pillow with a delighted chuckle.

"What's the matter?" mumbled Nancy from her pillow. She lay without moving but with her big eyes on Marjory's face. Marjory was glad her little sister was awake. Half the fun of a dream is telling about it.

"Oh, let me tell you, Nancy! I had the most wonderful dream. I thought the whole Sunday

School class was in Miss Louisa's wedding!" Nancy's eyes opened wider. Miss Louisa had at last settled on next month for her wedding and it was the chief topic of conversation with all the girls in her class. Some of them had never been to a wedding and few to a large church wedding, as this was to be. No wonder Marjory dreamed of it. "We were all bridesmaids and wore long dresses and you were flower girl and wore the tissue paper dress you wore in the play. But, oh, Nancy, you were barefooted!"

"I yam barefooted," murmured Nancy. She stuck out a foot from the bedclothes to prove it.

"But this was in church—right down the main aisle of Christ Church. But no one minded at all. Oh, wouldn't it be fun?" She sat thinking on the glories of the dream and the reality. She turned to Nancy but saw that she was asleep again. The quiet of the spring Sunday settled down. The household was sleeping late.

In the next room she could hear Emily stirring. Emily was supposed to live with Grandma but she spent a lot of time at the Cameron's house. Grandma had had company ever since they had returned from New Orleans and to Marjory's great joy Emily had stayed with them. She helped Marjory with her reading and made up wonderful games. But it seemed to Marjory that she wasted a lot of time on embroidery and primping. "I bet she's fixing her hair again now," Marjory scoffed to herself.

There was a matter that she must investigate, so Marjory hopped out of bed and went over to the blackboard that stood with the toys. Often there was a letter on it written by Fairy Jerome. After her disappointment about the ferryboat, Marjory had almost decided that fairies were "make-believe" when the letters, printed with bright colored chalk and full of fairy gossip, started and renewed her failing faith. She could imagine the tiny figure of a fairy, with the colored chalk held like a wand in her hand, flying in front of the blackboard, printing the big clear letters. She seemed to know just what the children had been doing and, nicest of all, she used words Marjory had learned to read. Sometimes just after Marjory had learned a word in school she would find it in the fairy's letter. It showed that the fairy was an educated person and Marjory was very careful to learn the words in her reader. Today's letter said,

> *Dear Marjory and Nancy:*
> *I came to see you last night. I rode on*
> *a squirrel.* [Friday at school Marjory had
> almost cried over the word "squirrel."
> Now she spelled it out proudly.] *The moon*
> *was up and I saw Marjory and Nancy in*
> *bed. I love you. Here are some kisses.*
>
> *Fairy Jerome*

And down on the chalk rack were the kisses—molasses candy kisses wrapped in silver paper. Marjory sucked hers thoughtfully. Fairy Jerome's kisses were like the ones that Emily made. A hazy idea began to rise in Marjory's mind. But just then she heard the bath water running in the tub and Mamma came to the door.

"Hurry and get your bath first, Marjory," she said. Marjory pattered down the hall to the bathroom as Mamma got out their clean clothes for Sunday School and Nancy stirred and stretched. When she came back steamy and rosy from her bath, Mamma buttoned her ferris

waist for her and left her to finish dressing
while she helped Nancy bathe.

"It is so warm I think you can leave off your
union suits," she said. Marjory buttoned on the
cool starched drawers. She was glad there were
no long union suit legs to bulge under her stockings. It made it much easier to dress. Her hair
that was braided through the week was up on
kid curlers and Mamma would fix it later. She
wouldn't risk her best dress at breakfast, so with
her pink kimono pinned at the neck, she sat and
watched Nancy being dressed. The Japanese
gong sounded for breakfast and they raced
downstairs, their kimonos standing out like
lampshades over their starched petticoats.

As they walked toward Sunday School later
the stiff petticoats were holding out stiff little
dresses. Marjory swished hers under her light
coat. Her dress was belted at the waist with a
pink sash and her round hat was covered with
flowers. Nancy still wore a "baby dress" that
hung straight from the shoulders and her hat
was a bonnet with a blue satin lining. They both
had purses made of polished and painted clam
shells. At least Nancy had hers. But as they
drew near the church Marjory said, "Nancy,

I've forgotten my purse with our collection money. I know just where it is—on the hatrack at home. I'll take you to the church and you go on to Miss Louisa's class. I'll get it and meet you there."

Marjory ran all the way home and back and was breathless when she returned. She hurried to a seat beside Miss Louisa and her group of little girls. Nancy was among them and talking at a rate unusual for her. Marjory sat at the end of the bench and fanned herself with her Sunday School leaflet. Suddenly with amazement and indignation she realized that Nancy was telling them her dream. "An' I was a flower girl an' I wore my blue paper dress an' I was barefooted." And then she added, "An' little flowers were growing on the carpet." "Oh, no, Nancy," corrected Marjory. "That wasn't in it." "I guess I know my own dream," frowned Nancy. "All of us were in it," she continued blandly to her audience.

Marjory was too astonished to speak. The nerve of Nancy to steal her dream! And right in church, too! She waited tense, to see if God Himself would punish the sinner. But Nancy went serenely on. Marjory sputtered, "It

wasn't that way! Let *me* tell it. I—I *know*—."
"Hush, dear," Miss Louisa said quietly. "She
is right. Let her tell her own dream." Before
Marjory could protest further the choir came
in singing the opening hymn and Sunday School
began. When opening service was over and each
teacher had gathered her class around her and
started the lesson Marjory turned to Miss
Louisa to explain. But what could she say? To
fuss in Sunday School about a dream seemed
silly and unimportant—and yet it was *her*
dream. *She* had seen the dim, misty figure of
the bride and all the children in a long, gay
procession; she had seen it in her dream. How
dared Nancy! And yet, how could Marjory, in
church, tell anyone that her little sister was not
telling the truth? She sat and worried and
boiled with anger and resentment. When she
was asked what her sponsors in baptism had
promised for her she forgot the exciting answer
about the Devil and all his works and said sul-
lenly that she didn't know. Somehow she got
through the morning and when the closing
hymn was finished she took Nancy's hand and
hurried toward home.

Anyone watching would have seen two dainty

little girls walking quietly home from Sunday School. Nancy was truly calm. She seemed to have nothing on her mind and looked up in amazement, when halfway home, Marjory burst out, "Oh, Nancy, how could you? You knew that was *my* dream. *I* dreamed it and you told everyone in church—*right in church*—that *you* did. That's the worst story I ever heard. That's stealing—stealing my dream."

"*My* dream," Nancy answered calmly, not at all upset.

Marjory gasped. Nancy was not going to admit that she was in the wrong! She sputtered with exasperation. Her voice became loud and excited.

"It's not! It's not!" she cried. "You took it! It's mine."

"It is not," answered Nancy, with maddening calm. "It's my dream. *I* dreamed it."

She walked on and Marjory followed her. She was furious but baffled. She must convince Nancy that this was her own dream, her own happy, lovely possession.

"Don't you remember, Nancy?" she said, trying to speak quietly. "I told you about it this morning in bed."

"No," said Nancy, looking at her Sunday School picture card. "I dreamed it all myself."

"Oh, Nancy, you know better!" Marjory burst into tears and ran ahead, leaving Nancy to follow her happy and unrepentant way.

Marjory wanted to run to Mamma and pour out her woes. But how could she prove what she was saying? If Nancy had taken her purse or her dress she could prove it was hers. Mamma would see it and know that it belonged to Marjory. *Everyone* would know it. And this dream was hers even more than a purse or dress! Hers alone! She wanted to scream out her rights. But even in her excitement she realized that Nancy's calm assertions sounded more true than her frenzied protests. She rushed in the front door and up to their room and flung herself on the bed.

"I won't say a word, not a word," Marjory determined as she heard Nancy coming upstairs. But as soon as she saw Nancy at the door she burst out again.

"Leave me alone! You robber! You stole my dream!"

"I'm not! I'm not," cried out Nancy, shaken

125

at last. "Mamma! Mamma! Marjory called me a robber!"

"What on earth is the matter?" Mamma dashed upstairs. Marjory was sobbing with her face in the pillow and Nancy was standing in the middle of the floor crying lustily.

Mamma sat down on the edge of the bed with her arm around Nancy. "What is it? What is it, my darlings?" she pleaded. Bit by bit she got the story—either Marjory had had a dream and Nancy claimed it or Nancy had had the dream and Marjory claimed it. It would have seemed ridiculous except for the two tragic little girls. She was as much in the dark as before.

"Oh, dear," she worried. "As if I did not have enough to do without deciding the ownership of dreams! One of you must be wrong, of course. Marjory, are you *sure?*"

The question showed Marjory how doubtful her whole story sounded. She burst into louder howls. Nancy was already crying hard but she added a little bit of extra noise to show that she was feeling every bit as bad as Marjory was. Mamma wasted no more time on talk. She called Emily to bathe Nancy's face and take her out in the hammock to quiet down. She helped Marjory to cool her hot face with some cologne and when she was quieter told her, "I don't think the matter of the dream is serious but I am worried because one of you is not telling the truth. I can't have this quarreling. I think you must stop talking to each other until this is cleared up."

"Oh, Mamma, you don't believe me!" Marjory nearly sobbed again.

Mamma gave her a quick hug. "I think I do, honey. And yet Nancy seems just as sure. Here, I'm going to let you use my chamois skin on your little red nose. Now, let's go down to dinner."

For Marjory the next few days were gray and dreary. She and Nancy kept the rule of silence but she was the only one who seemed troubled about it. Nancy had made up a game of selling violets that she found in the borders of the flower beds. She sold them, with leaves for money, to members of the family, to Pearl, to Jo when she came over on an errand, even to passersby. This kept her in constant conversation in contrast to Marjory's worried silence. Marjory went quietly to school and in the afternoon tagged after Emily like a sick puppy. She tried to write to Fairy Jerome because she felt that

that wise sprite would know the truth, but second reader words were not big enough for her feelings. Even the approach of Miss Louisa's wedding was dimmed by the shadow of the disputed dream.

On Friday morning Marjory woke early and lay blinking in the half light. She turned her eyes toward the blackboard as she did every morning to see if Fairy Jerome had left a letter there. She was an erratic fairy and sometimes the blackboard was bare of the colored letters. At first Marjory thought it was too dark to see anything in that corner. Then she realized that the blackboard was not there at all! This was amazing. As she lay sleepily wondering what had happened to it, she saw the door open slowly and Emily look in. She glanced at the beds, and quietly carried the blackboard in and set it up in its usual place. She knelt down and added a few words to the letter in colored chalk (Fairy Jerome's letter!) and then she tucked two little packages wrapped in tissue paper into the chalk rack.

Marjory lay quite still as Emily tiptoed out. She could not have said a word if she had wanted to. Now all the little half-doubts she had had

about the reality of Fairy Jerome were real and
sure. Emily had written all those letters. There
wasn't any Fairy Jerome at all! She felt as if
she had lost a lovely friend. As she lay there it
seemed too sad to be true. And yet there was
something comforting about Emily kneeling
there in the half-light and tucking away the little presents. How dear Emily had been about
this! She had helped Marjory so much that day
on the ferry and then, because she knew that her
faith in fairies was shaken, she had started the
letters from Fairy Jerome. After she had helped
Marjory with her reading she used the new
words in the letters each night. And when Marjory and Nancy had talked about their fairy
friend she had listened and encouraged them.
And think of all those presents she had given
from Fairy Jerome with no thought of thanks.
Emily was a dear! Marjory felt that all she
loved in Fairy Jerome was still there in Emily.
She wondered if she should tell Emily that she
knew the secret. Grown ups had so many secrets,
secrets to protect children or to make them hap-
pier. She snuggled down in her bed with a com-
fortable feeling for the first time in that terrible

week. She felt loved and cherished and secure.
And so she drifted to sleep.

When she woke again she looked over at the
blackboard. Fairy Jerome's letter was there.
Then she remembered. But was it true? Had
Emily come into the room with the blackboard
or had Marjory dreamed that? It seemed like a
dream. No, it had really happened. Suddenly,
like a flash of light, the solution of the "stolen
dream" came to her. *Nancy had had this same
feeling.* She had half-waked and heard Marjory
tell the dream, had gone back to sleep and waked
again, thinking *she* had dreamed it all herself!
Marjory understood it all now. She heard Papa
go singing down the hall to his bath. She slipped
quietly out of bed and into Mamma's room.

"Can I come in bed with you?" Mamma
reached out a hand. "Oh, Mamma, it's all
right!" she breathed as she cuddled down at
Mamma's side. "Nancy and I are both right. I
had the dream but Nancy truly believed she had
it." And she told her mother of the explanation
that had just come to her. She told about Fairy
Jerome too, but that was only important because it served to make the matter of the dream
clear.

"Why, of course! How stupid of me not to think of that. This was smart of you, Marjory. But, oh dear, now we have to explain it to Nancy. She is such a baby. Will we ever be able to do it?"

"Oh, we don't have to. If you and Papa know and *I* know, I don't care."

"Perhaps we ought to tell Miss Louisa," said Mamma slowly. "You both acted badly in Sunday School. Are you sure you don't mind not explaining to Nancy?"

"No, I'll *give* her the dream. It will be our secret, like grown-ups have."

"Then it's settled," Mamma said with a little pat. "And, Marjory, I think you are being very grown-up."

No one had ever said such a nice thing to Marjory before. As she happily got out of bed she thought of something that Emily had said and giggled. She turned back. "And just because Emily wrote those letters, it doesn't prove there aren't any fairies."

Mamma smiled at the "grown-up" Marjory.

"Certainly not," she said.

CHAPTER NINE

Miss Louisa's Wedding

THE MARJORY WHO came home from school Friday afternoon was a very different Marjory from the one of the past week. She felt gay and alive and trotted happily along, skipping on the brick sidewalk as if they were hop-scotch charts and swinging her books at the end of her book-strap recklessly.

Mr. Schumacher's grocery cart rattled by and she called and waved to him happily. She felt friendly with all the world. A mockingbird perched on a fence post just ahead of her and

132

spoke to her with a ripple of notes. Marjory
tried to answer him but her queer whistle drove
him away. Marjory laughed. He would come
back or another one would. The day seemed full
of spring and new beginnings. Although it was
afternoon and Easter was still some weeks away,
Marjory found herself singing *Welcome Happy
Morning!* to the time of her prancing steps.

Even when she turned in at her own gate she
kept up her tune, down the brick walk, up the
front steps and across the front gallery.

> *"Earth her joy confesses*
> *Clothing her for spring!"*

she shouted as she threw her books with a thump
on the hatrack.

"Marjory!" Mamma called from the parlor.
"Come on in here. Miss Louisa is here."

Marjory gave the little push up to her hair
ribbons that was her idea of making herself pre-
sentable and entered, grinning a little shyly. She
hoped that Mamma had already explained to
Miss Louisa about the dream. Miss Louisa
turned toward her and sang another line of the
song, "Loose the souls long prisoned." She
laughed as she put an arm around her. Marjory

wriggled happily. All explanations were over and Miss Louisa understood.

Mamma nodded toward a plate of cookies on the center table. Marjory took one and sat in the window seat and nibbled happily as Mamma and Miss Louisa went on talking.

"Well, the whole affair has shown me one thing," said Miss Louisa. "I would be selfish to have that wedding without including the Sunday School class somehow. Marjory's and Nancy's tale of the dream made me see how interested the whole class is."

"But, Louisa, twelve little girls! And your plans are all made. It is less than two weeks off, isn't it?" Mamma protested.

"Surely there is some place they could fit in." Miss Louisa frowned, thinking hard. "Could they tend the punch bowl at the reception?"

"Oh, no!" cried Marjory suddenly. They all laughed, for Marjory at the punch bowl presented such opportunities for disaster that they knew at once that was not the solution.

"I know! I know!" said Miss Louisa. "They can tend the ribbons that mark off the family pews! Three pews on each side of the center aisle and one girl at each end of each pew. Three times two times two, Marjory?"

"Twelve," said Marjory, not because she had worked it out, but because she knew there were twelve girls in the class.

"Can they be ready in time?" Mamma worried.

"They won't have to have special dresses—just white dresses with pink sashes," said Miss Louisa, thinking fast. "And I'll have some little bands of roses for their hair like Dot is wearing."

Marjory gasped. Dot Whiting, Mr. Bob's sister, was the flower girl. She reached for another cookie and listened absorbedly.

"Could Nancy manage a ribbon?" Mamma asked.

"Nancy could manage the whole wedding," Miss Louisa laughed. "But we could put the younger ones at the side aisles where they would be decorative but won't have so much to do. Most people will use the center aisle. Marjory, you must be in front, on my family's side because you started the whole thing." She smiled quickly at Marjory and then turned to Mamma.

"I wonder, if I gave you the list, would you

135

phone the other mothers for me. Keep it simple
—just the kind of dresses they have for Easter,
lawns, or linens or—oh, you know, not fancy.
I'm due now at the dressmaker's." She looked at
her watch and gathered up her gloves and purse.
She said "Good-bye" hurriedly and swept down
the walk. At the gate she turned. "Be *sure* to
keep it simple," she said.

Marjory wondered in the hectic days that
followed what it would have been like if it had
not been simple. There were endless phone calls
and consultations between mothers, and hurried
shopping trips. And there were the complicated
arrangements to be made about Katie Johnson,
the sewing woman who made children's clothes
for many of the little girls. In the end Mamma
gave up her days of Katie and she and Grandma
and Emily set to work on Marjory's dress. For-
tunately Nancy had had a hand embroidered
lawn sent her recently by Aunt Fan. By running pink ribbons instead of blue in the beading
and wider pink ribbon around the high waist it
would be perfect. Grandma had already started
Marjory's Easter dress and everyone worked on
it. It was white lawn with rows of tucks and
bands of lace set in the skirt and around the

neck. Mamma got her a sash of soft pink satin with tiny roses in the weave. When Marjory tried it on she thought of the "Lost Child" at the park last year. How she had envied her! She would not be "doll-like," she knew, but she hoped that nothing would happen to her this time.

The night of the rehearsal was exciting in itself. The wedding party gathered in the dim church to go through their parts for the big day. Marjory stood at the front left hand pew holding the cord that represented the ribbon. One of the bridesmaids showed her how to roll it up in her hand so that it would not drag on the floor.

"Oh, help me do it right tomorrow!" she prayed as she thought of her responsibility. She looked around. Pauline, across the aisle from her, rolled her cord up quickly and stood quietly. Nancy at the other end of her pew was big-eyed but calm. They watched as the maid of honor and two bridesmaids came slowly down the aisle to the softly played music. They looked queer in their street dresses. The flower girl wore a red coat. Miss Louisa directed from the pew where Marjory stood.

"Oh, I hope nothing happens to throw me off tomorrow," she said to Marjory. "I am ready to scream right now!"

"It will be all right," said Marjory and she felt it would be.

But she wasn't so sure the next day. She had slept on her kid curlers and had an excited and wakeful night. All morning she was restless. There wasn't anything to do about the wedding but the air was electric. After lunch Mamma made Marjory and Nancy lie down but they couldn't nap. They lay and whispered to each other and wondered every five minutes what time it was. But rest and baths and dinner were finally over and it was time to dress.

Emily arrived all dressed for the wedding just as the florist delivered their wreaths of tiny pink roses. She brought them upstairs. "You help Marjory, won't you, Emily?" said Mamma. "I'll take Nancy in my room and dress her."

"I am not going to try to curl your hair in ringlets," said Emily as she removed the kid curlers. Marjory watched in the mirror with interest as she brushed it sleekly smooth at the top and fluffed the ends in a soft light cloud.

She tied a narrow band of pink ribbon under the back and pinned the bandeau of roses to it across the front.

"Oh, Emily, it looks lovely," said Marjory. "And it feels tight. I won't have to worry about hair ribbons falling off and curls coming out."

"Two worries removed," laughed Emily. "I'll try to make you as snug as possible. Everything you're wearing is new and should be just right—petticoat the right length, new garters that will hold your stockings smooth." She checked over carefully. "And," drawing the soft lacy dress over Marjory's head, "your dress is perfect!"

She tied the wide pink sash around Marjory's waist and then sewed it tightly through the knot. "I *dare* that sash to come untied," she said. As a finishing touch she stuck two handkerchiefs under the sash, one on each side.

"Marjory, you are all secure and you look perfectly lovely," she said. "Not a thing can happen. Now stop worrying!"

Marjory laughed as she looked at herself in the mirror. Emily had understood again and come to the rescue. She turned and gave her a butterfly kiss. "Careful of your dress!" said

Emily with a parting pat. Marjory felt light-hearted and as calm as Nancy as she climbed into the surrey to drive to the church. Papa was taking them early and would come back for Mamma and Emily. Nancy looked darling with her smooth dark curls and little rose wreath in her hair. Marjory thought of the dream that had caused so much trouble and yet had also caused this happiness. She squeezed Nancy's hand.

"It is better than your dream, isn't it?" she whispered.

"What dream?" asked Nancy and then looked around curiously when Marjory laughed and laughed. "All that worry!" Marjory thought.

A few people were beginning to arrive as Marjory and Nancy took their places at either end of the left-hand front pew. Pauline was already in place across the aisle and whispered, "You look lovely," to Marjory. "So do you," Marjory whispered back. She felt gracious and charming and confident. This was really simple, and fun.

Gradually the church filled. Miss Louisa's relatives from out of town were shown into the

second and third pews. Marjory heard them
rustle in behind her, with whiffs of rose and
violet perfumes that mingled with the waxy
odor of the candles glowing up near the altar.
The organist began playing softly. How lovely
the old church was at night with the tall brass
vases of white roses gleaming in the light and
the carved wood screen around the choir stalls
like dark lace. Only the stained glass windows
that were so colorful by day were dull and life-
less at night. They would be gleaming from the
outside like jewels, though. It was so dreamlike
that Marjory almost forgot her task. Then the
usher led Miss Louisa's mother to the pew.
Marjory lifted the ribbon and rolled it up cor-
rectly. With a rustle of her lilac silk gown,
Mrs. Leonard was seated. She smiled as Marjory
slipped back the ribbon. There was room for the
uncle who would give Miss Louisa away but
most of Marjory's task was over.

The music, which had been playing softly,
changed to the rich strains of the Lohengrin
march—"Here comes the bride." The minister
and Mr. Bob Whiting and the best man took
their places up in front and the wedding procession began. Marjory standing at her post could

not turn to look but others did; she could hear them in a soft silken wave. She could only wait as the slow procession came down the aisle and see them as they passed her. She paid no attention to the ushers. Her eyes were on the bridesmaids. Their dresses were of softest pink chiffon, shirred and ruffled and trailing in long trains on the ruby red carpet. Their hats were softly pink, too, and wreathed in deeper pink roses like those in their graceful "shower" bouquets.

"They are like queens," thought Marjory. It was impossible to think of these dignified creatures as the girls who had laughed and chattered at the rehearsal. As they took their places the maid of honor followed, in deeper pink and with darker roses. Then the flower girl in white lace over pink and a pink wreath in her hair, "like mine," thought Marjory happily. And then finally came The Bride—all in white satin with white roses and a misty veil that spread out like a cloud behind her. But this fairy princess was still Miss Louisa and she gave Marjory the tiniest flicker of a smile as she passed her.

"Dearly beloved, we are gathered here—"

Marjory was in a happy daze as the minister
began the ceremony. In a daze she admitted the
uncle after he had given away the bride, in a
daze she heard the vows. And then, just as the
Mendelssohn march started and the maid of
honor was arranging the bride's veil to come
back down the aisle, it happened—the terrible
something that Marjory had feared all along.
Just outside of the pew where Marjory was
sitting there appeared a tiny mouse. Marjory
choked back a scream. She was terribly afraid.
For a moment she thought of kicking at it—
anything to get it away from her! But then it
would run toward the wedding party. She remembered Miss Louisa saying long ago at the
party, "Once I fainted when there was just a
tiny mouse." Suppose she should faint now! She
mustn't! She mustn't! And Marjory was the
only one who could do anything. She reached
quietly into her sash for a handkerchief, for
two handkerchiefs! She spread them out on her
hand and quickly leaned over and picked up
the little mouse! The procession was starting
from the altar and no one noticed her. She stood
erect at once and held her hands together over
the mouse. It was terrible to feel him scratching

and wriggling through the two handkerchiefs. What could she do now? The wedding procession filled the aisle. Should she let him go when they were past? He might scurry down the aisle. But could she wait for the slow procession? The wriggling body in her hands gave a sudden jump and for a minute she thought she would have to let go. "I won't! I won't!" she muttered to herself but she was trembling with revulsion and fear.

The music was not quite as slow as the entrance music and the bridal party moved faster now. But it seemed an eternity until each one passed; the bride and groom, and slowly, slowly, the attendants.

As the last one passed her, Marjory determined to get out at once. She stepped out in the aisle behind the bridal party and followed slowly down the aisle with her wriggling burden. Miss Louisa's uncle saw her go but thought it must be some part of the ceremony he had not been told of. Mamma and Papa and Emily saw her and whispered loudly to stop her. The congregation gasped. Those who knew her wondered what had gotten into shy little Marjory Cameron. She *never* made scenes!

Marjory paid no attention to anyone. "Just to get out!" was her only thought. Halfway down the aisle the desperate little animal in her hands grew quiet. But she could feel his heart thump, thump, thumping under her fingers. "Poor thing!" she thought. "He is frightened, too," and she stroked his back with one finger. "There, there," she murmured. "I'm not going to hurt you—just let you loose." Suddenly she was no longer frightened. But she was still determined to protect Miss Louisa. This perfect wedding must not be spoiled.

At last! Here she was at the vestibule! The wedding party was clustered there but she pushed past them and put the mouse down on the steps. He blinked for a minute dazedly and did not move.

"Here, kid!" cried one of the ushers. "What kind of a trick is this?" Marjory stood in embarrassed silence. But Miss Louisa saw the mouse as he ran out into the dark and realized what had happened.

"Oh, Marjory, darling! You brave person! Don't scold her! She just saved my wedding! Oh, honey, weren't you scared to death?" Down

on her knees she went, white satin and veil and
all and gathered Marjory in her arms.

"Yes'm, I was scared but he was too," Marjory said against the tulle.

The guests were beginning to come out and
Miss Louisa and Mr. Bob ran to their carriage.
They were going to the bride's home for the
reception.

"One of you bring Marjory with you," the
bride called to the bridesmaids. "I might need
her for protection!"

And that is what happened. The maid of
honor left word for Papa and Mamma and took
Marjory in the cab with her.

When Marjory got to the reception Miss
Louisa, Mrs. Whiting now, made her tell everything that had happened. And as the guests
came up to them with good wishes Miss Louisa
repeated the story again and again. "Just imagine picking up that dreadful little beast," she
said. "I might have stumbled on him or tan-
gled him in my veil!" She told Marjory to
stand close to them as they received their guests,
"to guard us," she said with a smile.

Marjory laughed and forgot to be shy in the
midst of the joyful confusion. And then, to top

it all, she saw Papa and Mamma coming toward them.

"What has this child been doing now?" asked
Papa, half anxiously.

"This child has been wonderful!" Miss
Louisa said and told the story all over again.

"I'm glad you kept your head, Marjory,"
said Mamma quietly.

"*And* a clean handkerchief!" grinned Papa
but Marjory saw that their eyes were proud.